The war created some strange things. But Augustus certainly wasn't complaining. The clothing outlined her lithe body quite nicely. As she turned and leaned over to pick up the fireplace poker and stirred up the flames, Augustus gasped. The lady was not only well-bred, she was beautiful.

He hadn't noticed that Villars was standing up again and had taken his arm. The elderly man turned and followed his gaze.

"Ready?" Augustus asked absently, keeping his eyes on the girl.

When the man didn't respond, Augustus looked over at him. Villars was still as a statue as he stared at the lady in the parlor.

Except for the man's fingers digging into his arm, Augustus would have thought Villars had turned to stone.

"Are you alright?"

The man's eyes bulged. Augustus shook him gently. "Villars? Are you well?"

"No sir," Villars said in a whisper.

The girl must have heard them. The poker still her hand, she turned and looked at them. They must have looked quite a sight – the tall sturdy soldier and the frail black man clutching his arm, both staring wide-eyed at her.

Her eyes focused on Augustus.

"I apologize, ma'am." Augustus forced his eyes away from

her briefly, then back. It was impolite to stare, but looking at her was like looking at a beautiful painting. "I didn't know there was a lady here."

She didn't answer, but instead placed her free hand on the mantle.

Villars drew in a sharp intake of breath and straightened to his full height. "Miss Arabella."

ONCE IN A BLUE MOON

ALSO BY KATHRYN KALEIGH

THE BECQUERELS

Twist of Fate

When the Stars Align

Once in a Blue Moon

Once Upon a Christmas

A Wish Upon a Star

Written in the Wind

Scripted in the Stars

Destined in the Twilight

Promised in the Mist

Trapped in the Melody

When Lightning Strikes

Storm of Time

Midnight Storm

When the Moon Falls

Stormborn Angel

Time Tempest

The Heart Remembers

A Moment in Time

Moonlight Shadows

Rescued in Time

ONCE IN A BLUE MOON

THE BECQUERELS

KATHRYN KALEIGH

To learn more about Kathryn Kaleigh, visit

www.kathrynkaleigh.com

Kathryn Kaleigh

PROLOGUE

As Arabella Becquerel unfolded the letter in her hands, the faded parchment paper crinkled beneath her fingertips. She slid her toes out of her black pumps. Then glancing at the attorney watching her as he finished up a phone call at his desk across the room, slid her foot back into her shoe.

She was confused by the formality of her great-grandmother Vaughn's estate attorney. When her great-grandfather Jonathan died fourteen months ago, the estate had seamlessly passed to her great-grandmother. That was when Arabella learned that Jonathan had put everything he owned in Vaughn's name before they were even married – before his last deployment to Vietnam.

After Jonathan had died peacefully in his sleep at the age of eighty-four, the light had gone out of her great-grandmother's eyes. Arabella was convinced that Vaughn had died of a broken heart. Takotsubo cardiomyopathy.

Arabella's cell phone blinked with a text message. She glanced at her phone resting next to her on the plush dark brown sofa.

How much longer?

Her fiancé, Matthew Caldwell Jennings, III, had been miffed when she'd asked him to wait in the lobby. Even though she was engaged to be married to him and he was an attorney to boot, it hadn't felt right to have him there when the attorney went over Vaughn's estate.

It was something Arabella wanted – needed – to do alone.

Ignoring Matthew's impatience, she opened the letter and blinked back a fresh wave of tears as she recognized her great-grandmother's handwriting.

My dearest Arabella,

Right about now, you're going to be wondering at the mystery surrounding my estate.

Arabella would have smiled under other circumstances. Instead, she swallowed the lump in her throat. Taking a deep breath, she continued reading.

There are things – so many things – I haven't told you. As you read this letter, you'll have a better understanding about why I worked so hard to instill a love of history in you. Why history is so interwoven in our shared blood.

Arabella's eyes blurred with moisture and she put a hand over her eyes. Her throat burned as a sob escaped her fragile self-control. Her tears fell on the paper and smudged the ink of Vaughn's signature at the bottom of letter. Arabella gasped when she noticed her tears on the paper. She wiped at the letter, but only succeeded in smudging the ink and blurring Vaughn's words.

CHAPTER 1

urn right in one hundred feet.

Arabella turned onto what looked more like a footpath than a road. "Seriously?" She muttered to herself.

Having grown up in the urban world of Baton Rouge, Louisiana, it was baffling that her great-grandmother had lived here in the countryside outside of Natchez until taking Arabella to raise thirty years ago. It was only more baffling that Arabella didn't know this until after her great-grandmother's death.

She pulled up in front of the house and turned off the motor. The house was a quintessential antebellum mansion. Huge pillars lined the balcony that ran along the whole outside edge of the house. Tall French windows/doors ran from floor to ceiling. The white paint was fresh and spring flowers spilled from pots on the veranda. Unbeknownst to Arabella until three weeks ago, her grandparents had paid a neighbor to keep the house up.

For thirty years.

Her great-grandmother, it seemed, had a surreptitious talent in financial matters.

Her heart ached as she walked up the steps to stand at the front door. She was pretty sure she was the reason her grandparents had moved from here to Baton Rouge, though the reason was lost somewhere within the smudged words of Vaughn's letter to her.

Holding the key in her hand, she hesitated. It was surreal that this house now belonged to her.

She gasped as the door opened, her feet frozen as she fought the urge to run back to the safety of her car. Who could be here in this abandoned house?

A man, maybe mid-sixties, opened the door and grinned at her. "You must be Arabella."

"Yes." She managed to keep her feet planted securely in place. And put what she hoped passed for a smile on her face.

"I'm Jerry."

Ah. The caretaker. "You live here then?"

His eyes widened sheepishly. "Only temporarily. My house flooded out and I needed a place to stay while I basically rebuilt it. My wife is staying with her sister in Jackson. It didn't seem right for us both to be living here."

"It's quite alright," Arabella assured him. "A house breathes better with someone inside."

He sighed with relief. "I didn't get a chance to run it by your great-grandmother on account of her taking sick and all." He lowered his eyes. "I sure am sorry to hear of her passing."

Arabella swallowed the lump in her throat and said the words that were expected. By now they were automatic. "Thank you. It means a lot to me for you to say so."

"Come on in here." Jerry opened the door wide for her to follow him inside.

She stepped into the foyer onto the polished mahogany floor reflecting light from the chandelier above. An odd sense of familiarity swept through her.

She walked to a nearly black rosewood grandfather clock

standing next to the staircase and studied its faded dial. The case was decorated with ornate columns. The clock's face wore a jagged rip between the Roman numerals six and seven.

She opened the little glass door and ran her fingertips along the rip.

"I apologize. What?" She realized Jerry was talking, but instead of turning toward him, she kept her gaze on the clock. It was silent. "Is it broken?"

"Oh no. That scar's been there since the Civil War."

"No. The clock. It isn't ticking."

"It's over two hundred years old, but I don't think it's broken. It needs winding, but I don't know where the key is."

Arabella tugged on a platinum chain she wore around her neck and pulled a key from beneath her sweater. She swept the chain over her head, inserted the key, and wound the clock.

"How did you…?" Jerry stopped talking and stood silently as she closed the glass door and the clock began to tick.

"Much better." She said, looking around now. "You were saying?"

"Never mind. If you're going to be staying for awhile, I can make other arrangements."

She turned and met his gaze. "There's no need for that. It's a big house. You'll hardly even know I'm here."

She went up the stairs and stopped on the landing to look out the wavy glass of the eight-foot-high window. The evening sun drifted over the tall pine trees that started a few yards past the lawn. Someone, probably Jerry, kept the lawn manicured. She placed one hand on the thick indigo French brocade draperies tied back on either side. Leaning her forehead against the smooth wooden frame, she rested her eyes.

Her great-grandmother Vaughn had always been prone to flights of fancy. Since Arabella was a child, she had told her tales of the south when the south was in its prime. When men and their ladies attended grand balls, waltzing beneath the moonlight.

What she hadn't told Arabella was that she owned a southern antebellum home. This was no doubt where Jonathan had come when he'd gone on *hunting trips.* Hunting trips that didn't seem to involve any hunting.

Yet her great-grandmother stayed away from here and went to extremes to keep Arabella away.

Jerry followed her up the stairs. "Miss Arabella. There's something else."

Turning, she looked at Jerry who was rubbing the beard on his chin. "What is it?" She smiled. He seemed like a nice man, but he was a nervous sort. "What is it Jerry?"

"Before my house flooded, I'd started renovating the bedrooms. About the time I got everything pulled out, my house flooded, so I haven't gotten back to it. I have some neighbors willing to help if need be, but the renovations are taking longer than I expected. So I'm sleeping in one of the rooms upstairs."

"Okay," Arabella said and continued upstairs.

"So there really isn't any place for you to sleep."

She stopped, looking down the stairs at him. "It's okay. I'll make do." She went upstairs and peeked into each bedroom, one by one. Just as Jerry had warned, the bedrooms were in disarray. All the furniture and art work had been moved into one room. One daybed had been left accessible and the bedding had been left thrown back and a little 12-inch television sat balanced on a chair next to the bed. This was obviously where Jerry was sleeping.

In the remaining rooms, the floors and light fixtures were covered in plastic, the windows and wall outlets were lined with painter's tape, and all the doors had been removed. One room had a set of sawhorses set up and a table saw and other tools as well as planks of wood to replace sections that were damaged.

"These are serious renovations." Without turning, she knew he was behind her, waiting in the hallway.

"I know." His voice held notes of apology. "Miss Vaughn met me in town before she took ill. She wouldn't come near the house, but I showed her pictures of what needed to be done. She knew every inch of this house."

"It's a travesty she didn't come back here."

"Yeah, do you know what happened?"

"I wish I did," Arabella said. "Would you be a dear and find me some bedding? I'll sleep in the parlor."

When he went off to search for bedding, she blew out her breath and walked through the master bedroom. She fervently wished that she could have spent time here with her great-grandparents, Jonathan and Vaughn. The true reason of why they never brought her here and why Vaughn never came near the house may forever be a mystery.

This was her house now and she intended to live here. Eventually.

But... there was much to be done first.

As she turned from the room, she noticed a storm brewing in the distance. The dark clouds were banked among the tips of the tall oak trees.

A flash of lightening was followed seconds later by a rumble of thunder. She shivered.

CHAPTER 2

Colonel Augustus Townsend stood on the veranda of the plantation house and watched as his men turned what had been immaculate grounds into a Confederate camp replete with tents, fires, and horses everywhere.

They'd ridden hard for three days. The horses needed to rest. The Union forces were tightening their ranks around Vicksburg. Augustus needed to get his men there before the fighting started, but they were still a full four day's march out.

Augustus was Southern through and through. He'd grown up in the South and with the exception of three years at West Point, he'd lived his entire life in the south. His job as a soldier was to protect the people of the south – his people. As far as he was concerned, that was the whole point of this damnable war.

Behind the house looked like a refugee camp. As they passed through small towns and farms on their northern trek from New Orleans to Vicksburg, he saw it as his duty to warn the people that the war was coming to their doorstep.

Most of the war was to their east - Atlanta, West Virginia - he'd give them that, but the war was here, too. Without soldiers to protect them, the people would be exposed. He encouraged them to follow his troops to Vicksburg. Once they were safely there, he and General Pemberton's men together, could defeat the enemy. On the ground of their choosing.

In the hour since their arrival, Augustus had determined that this house belonged to Charles and Erika Becquerel. Charles was fighting – somewhere - and his wife had gone to stay for the duration of the war in New Orleans with her sister-in-law.

Nonetheless, the house was teaming with people. The Becquerels appeared to be his kindred spirits. They turned no one away from their door, including the servants that they had set free.

He'd told the older black man, Villars, that they should pack their necessary things and go to Vicksburg. He'd said they would consider it. Thirty minutes later, the house was rife with people carrying who-knew-what here and there.

One thing he'd learned in his travels as a soldier – there was no accounting for what people deemed *necessary items.*

CHAPTER 3

"The Yankees are coming!"

Arabella stirred on the couch in the parlor. She was dreaming a most peculiar dream.

"Mistress, get up, the Yankees are coming."

Arabella opened her eyes and stared into the deep brown eyes of a dark skinned young woman wearing a long dress and scarf wrapped around her head.

With a quick glance around the room, she realized she was in the parlor of the house bequeathed to her by her great-grandparents.

Her host, Jerry, hadn't said he was having visitors, but then Arabella hadn't asked.

The look in the woman's wide eyes, though, was nearly hysterical.

"What Yankees?" Arabella sat up, pulling the blanket securely around her shoulders.

"Mistress, I ain't knowing who you are, but it don't make no never mind. We's packing up now and we be leaving at first light."

Perhaps the woman had some type of psychosis. Arabella

saw this kind of thing from time to time in her work at the hospital. Unfortunately, Arabella didn't have any Haldol with her.

Someone scurried past, behind them. It was then that Arabella noticed that the woman standing over her wasn't the only person showing signs of hysteria. Men, women, and children, black and white, were rushing to and fro carrying items of dubious content around the house.

"It looks disorganized." She muttered to herself.

"Don't say I didn't warn ya." The woman turned and hurried off toward the foyer.

Arabella sat in awe as she watched the people rushing about. All she could think was that they were in serious need of triage training. She wondered if anyone knew what anyone else was doing.

She needed to find Jerry to see what was going on. Perhaps this was part of the renovation process. If so, it certainly explained why it was taking so long. *Longer than expected,* he'd said.

She reached into her pocket and pulled out her cell phone. She'd forgotten to call Matthew, her fiancé, last night to let him know that she'd arrived safely.

It was just as well. Her phone was barely charged and the words *No Service* made it clear that she wouldn't be calling anyone.

CHAPTER 4

ugustus needed sleep. He had no one to blame but himself for his lack thereof. After all, he'd been the one to encourage the people to pack up and go with them. Between the people running up and down the hallway, chattering about this and that, and moving of trunks, it was as loud outside his bedroom as it was in a tent with his men preparing for battle.

Besides, a commanding officer would never sleep while his men readied for battle.

Augustus groaned and climbed out of the most comfortable bed he'd lain in since he'd left home two years ago to fight in this war.

He pulled on his trousers and a white shirt. After tucking in his shirt, he pulled on his boots and tightened the laces. One of the frayed pieces snapped. Without a hitch, he tied the two ends together, adding another knot to his laces. He'd given his army-issued extra pair of laces to one of his men weeks ago.

By the time he was dressed, much of the hubbub in the hallway had subsided. He'd hardly reached the top of the stairs, when the elderly man, Villars, that he'd spoken to earlier, seemed to step from the shadows.

"Can I get something for you, Sir?" Villars leaned on his cane.

"No. No. I heard the commotion and thought I could be of assistance."

"Oh yes sir. The people are a mite anxious to be ready to go with you all first thing in the morning."

"I'm glad to hear that." Augustus took a step.

"I should be down there myself, but my old knees don't hold up on these stairs no more. Once I get up here for bed, I try not go back down 'til morning."

"Can I help you down?"

"Oh no, Sir. I couldn't impose." Villars shook his head.

"Don't be ridiculous." Augustus held out his arm. "Come on."

"If you insist, though it's not fitting."

"It's my pleasure."

Villars laid his hand on Augustus' arm and with Augustus taking most of his weight, they made it down to the landing, Villars rested a couple of minutes, then they started down the second part of the stairway.

"I need to rest another minute." Villars sat down five steps from the bottom. "These old knees ain't worth a darn anymore."

After helping the older man sit, Augustus leaned back against the railing and noticed that he had a good view into the parlor.

He saw a young lady standing in front of the fireplace. He'd been told the mistress of the house was in New Orleans. He hadn't been informed of any other ladies in the house. Just from her silhouette, he could see that she was a well-bred lady. But she wore what looked like denim trousers and a man's blue undershirt.

The war created some strange things. But Augustus certainly wasn't complaining. The clothing outlined her lithe body quite nicely. As she turned and leaned over to pick up the fireplace poker and stirred up the flames, Augustus gasped. The lady was not only well-bred, she was beautiful.

He hadn't noticed that Villars was standing up again and had taken his arm. The elderly man turned and followed his gaze.

"Ready?" Augustus asked absently, keeping his eyes on the girl.

When the man didn't respond, Augustus looked over at him. Villars was still as a statue as he stared at the lady in the parlor.

Except for the man's fingers digging into his arm, Augustus would have thought Villars had turned to stone.

"Are you alright?"

The man's eyes bulged. Augustus shook him gently. "Villars? Are you well?"

"No sir," Villars said in a whisper.

The girl must have heard them. The poker still her hand, she turned and looked at them. They must have looked quite a sight – the tall sturdy soldier and the frail black man clutching his arm, both staring wide-eyed at her.

Her eyes focused on Augustus.

"I apologize, ma'am." Augustus forced his eyes away from her briefly, then back. It was impolite to stare, but looking at her was like looking at a beautiful painting. "I didn't know there was a lady here."

She didn't answer, but instead placed her free hand on the mantle.

Villars drew in a sharp intake of breath and straightened to his full height. "Miss Arabella."

CHAPTER 5

*A*rabella tore her gaze from the handsome man standing on the stairs to the frail black man leaning against him.

Her name whispered by him floated across the room.

She frowned. The man looked vaguely familiar, but she couldn't place him.

Her eyes snapped back to the younger man. He was about her age, maybe just over thirty. Short dark hair. Clean shaven. A white shirt loose at the collar.

His gaze was pinned to hers. The black man slid down and sat on the stairs, putting his hands over his face.

Someone knocked on the front door. When Arabella didn't move to answer it, the man glanced around, then went to answer it himself.

Arabella couldn't see into the foyer, but their voices carried.

"Colonel Townsend?"

"Yes?"

"Sir I have news. May we speak privately?"

The front door closed and she could hear their muffled voices coming from the front veranda. *Colonel?* The man must be in the military then. He wasn't wearing a uniform, but of course he wouldn't be in uniform in the middle of the night.

Arabella had never had any interest in politics. She didn't have a TV, didn't read a newspaper, and rarely listened to the radio. The only news she got was through an app on her phone. Was there a war going on that she didn't know about? An invasion of some kind?

Her great-grandmother Vaughn's influence often sent her down a fanciful line of thinking, but she batted the irrational thoughts off like flies.

Arabella Becquerel's life was grounded in scientific logic.

Until three weeks ago, she had done little other than eat, sleep, and breath psychology. In fact, she couldn't remember ever having had a conversation with her fiancé that didn't involve something related to psychology. She'd try in vain to listen when he talked about law, but she was pretty sure her eyes glazed over with disinterest at least half the time.

Arabella turned and put the poker back in its stand. In the hour or so since she'd woken to chaos, things had quietened somewhat.

With the exception of the black man sitting on the stairs, staring at her again, everyone had disappeared, perhaps to sleep after their miserable attempt to triage whatever travel they were preparing for.

She'd heard the word Yankees more than once, but decided it was either some role play thing at best or a Folie a deux at worst. Whatever it was, she chose to stay uninvolved. She was only here to become acquainted with and begin making decisions about the property secretly owned by the grandparents who raised her.

The frail older man stood up and, using his cane, made his way toward her. He stopped a couple of feet in front of her. Arabella looked into his eyes, wise with age.

"Arabella. You've come back to us."

CHAPTER 6

ugustus stood in front of his second in command. "We have to stay here."

"What? We can't." The soldier straightened and cleared his throat. "I apologize. I mean, Sir. What about Vicksburg?"

"No need to apologize, Beau. It's out of my hands. Vicksburg will have to wait. Unfortunately, we need to batten down here. It seems the Federals have stopped at the port and dumped a regime of soldiers off to hit Vicksburg from the east. We're sitting right in their path."

Beau's adam apple bobbed. "Yes sir."

"At ease, Beau. I'm gonna need you with me on this. Since I'm the only doctor here, I may be otherwise occupied if there are wounded."

Before he caught himself, Beau's lips twitched up at the prospect of assuming command of their soldiers. Augustus sighed. Did the young never tire of pursuing the thrill of glory? "Go on," He said, his voice weary. "Get the men up so we can give them the news."

Beau turned and started around toward the back of the house where the soldiers had pitched their tents. The young soldier had a lightness in his step that Augustus hadn't seen in months.

Augustus just wanted to go home. To have this war over and return to his family in Jefferson county. He was so close now. Even though he was next to the wide Mississippi River, the air smelled more like home than any he'd breathed in months. There was still a chance he could take a few days to slip home to see his folks. Augustus was having trouble remembering a world where there was no war. The country would be permanently scared now. He only hoped that in two hundred years, this folly would still be remembered. Otherwise, so many lives would have been lost in vain.

His brother was somewhere – Gettysburg fighting his own battle for the south. His father had died before this war even started. Augustus could only pray that the women-folk were getting along without them.

Augustus ran a hand through his hair and looked back at the house. So many lives upended from this damnable war. Take this family, for instance. The husband was off fighting and the wife was displaced.

All Augustus wanted to do was to get home, find a wife and have some children. Practice medicine. And live a normal life.

His attention was drawn to a window of the house. Someone was staring out into the darkness. It was the young lady he'd seen standing near the fireplace. She was silhouetted by the lantern in the background. His heart did a little stutter. She was beautiful. In fact, she was the most beautiful woman he had ever seen. It had been years – since the war started - since he'd been interested in talking with a female. But this woman…

He wanted to talk to her. To find out if she was as beautiful up close as she was from a distance. To find out if she could hold an engaging conversation.

Even before the war, he had given up on finding someone

who was both interesting to talk to and delightful to look at. So much so that he'd thrown himself into his studies and given up pursuit of a wife - to the chagrin of his mother.

He pulled his gaze away from her and walked around to the back of the house to inform his men of the change in plans.

The war was making him addled.

Now was not the time to be thinking of finding a wife.

CHAPTER 7

*A*rabella's training was automatic. "Please. Let me help you sit." When he didn't protest, she led the frail man to the nearest sofa and helped him sit. "Do we know each other?"

The man blinked, looked into her eyes, and seemed to regain some of his senses. "Of course not. My name is Villars."

Arabella held out her hand. "It's nice to meet you Villars."

He looked at her hand, then back to her face, his eyes wide.

She smiled encouragingly, trying to put him at ease. He put his fingers lightly against hers, and bent his head over the back of her hand, then released her hand.

"Welcome home," he said.

"Thank you." Arabella wasn't sure how to take this man. Perhaps he was merely from an older generation with outdated customs, but somehow he seemed to know about her. Perhaps Jerry had told him. "Do you know where Jerry is?"

"Jerry?" The word sounded strange on his lips. His gaze met hers again with an intensity that reminded Arabella of a fortune teller Vaughn had taken her to one time in New Orleans. The memory still sent shivers down her spine.

Time is an illusion. The fortune teller had looked up from her crystal ball to peer into Arabella's eyes. *For you more so than others.*

Arabella, thirteen years old at the time, had giggled until she saw her great-grandmother's stricken expression.

The fortune teller gazed into the ball again. *I see... destruction... I see...* The fortune teller frowned. *Your father's life... is in peril.*

Arabella had scoffed. Her parents had died shortly after her birth.

The fortune teller had closed her eyes. Swayed. Then opened her eyes and stared at Arabella as though she'd seen a ghost. *Leave me. I never want to see you again.*

Her great-grandmother had taken Arabella by the hand and dragged her from the fortune teller's tent. They had never talked about it again.

Arabella shook off the memory. It had been so long ago. Yet, she had never shaken the feeling of foreboding she'd felt leaving that tent.

"How do you know me?" She whispered, her voice catching.

The black man straightened his shoulders. "Your mother, Mistress Ericka, lives here."

CHAPTER 8

ugustus trudged back to the house. His men were disappointed and rightly so. After weeks of futility, they'd been looking forward to having a purpose. Protecting Vicksburg had given them something worthwhile to look forward to.

Instead, they were forced to batten down here and focus on protecting themselves from attack.

Such was the way of war.

In the meantime, Augustus found himself distracted by the beautiful young lady in the parlor. Villars had had a strange reaction to her. Almost like he recognized her, but it had been more like he'd seen a ghost. He called her Arabella. Was she a ghost then? Someone he'd known who had passed away and now reappeared?

Augustus shivered. He shook his head. It was more likely that he hadn't seen her in quite some time.

Besides, Villars was quite old and had trouble getting around. Perhaps his memory had lapsed.

Augustus went up the back stairs, shook the dirt off his boots, and went inside the back door. It was dark inside the house now and he made his way toward the stairway guided by moonlight and the muted glow from the fireplace.

When he reached the stairway, he stopped and looked to the left into the parlor. The pull was too strong for him to resist. He sat on the bottom step, untied his boots and slipped them off. Wearing only his socks, holes and all, he quietly padded over to the sofa to see if the girl was there.

His breath came in sharply when he saw her. She was asleep on the sofa, tucked beneath a blanket. He stepped closer and bent over to better see her. She looked real enough. Her slow steady breath belied any possibility that she was a ghost.

He didn't know how it was even possible, but she was more beautiful up close than from a distance. Her dark hair splayed across the pillow and his fingers itched to sweep aside a strand that lay across her cheek. Her full red lips were slightly parted in sleep and her dark lashes lay against flawless porcelain skin.

Augustus had never experienced love at first sight and typically scoffed at the whole idea, but he couldn't ignore the unfamiliar twist in his gut or the dryness in his mouth. He wanted to touch her so badly it was painful.

The beauty of southern women was known around the world as unsurpassed, and Augustus had met his share of beauties. But this one overshadowed them all.

She stirred and he jerked back. It would be difficult to explain standing over her. In fact, she would probably never speak to him due to his forward and ungentlemanly behavior.

Leaving her, he went back to the stairway and made his way up to his room.

Now that the house was quiet, perhaps he could get some sleep. Tomorrow he and his men would be up at first light to begin preparing the house to be a fortress. Especially now that he had Arabella to protect, he would do whatever it took to make sure they were safe from the Yankees.

CHAPTER 9

*A*rabella opened her eyes and gazed into the shadows. She was alone with only the embers of the fire in the hearth.

She'd been dreaming then. She'd sensed someone standing over her. Pulling the blanket under her chin, she gazed into the fireplace.

Her great-grandmother would have a fanciful explanation, but Arabella would have none of it. Dreams were merely her brain's efforts to prune itself of unneeded cells. Housekeeping of the mind. Her scientific studies had stripped any fanciful notions her great-grandmother had given her growing up and left her with streamlined, no nonsense thinking. Neurons and hormones. The brain only did what it was told.

Nonetheless, she couldn't deny the sensation that someone had stood over her.

I don't believe in ghosts.

If she did believe in ghosts, this house would be the place to see them.

Villars' words played in her head. *Your mother, Ericka lives here.*

Her great-grandmother had spoken often of Arabella's mother – Ericka. She shivered. Ericka had died when Arabella was an infant. Of course she didn't live here.

It was nonsense.

The man was old and had some difficulties with his memory. It was common at his age and nothing to be concerned about.

Arabella was exhausted. She rarely slept this much. As a psychologist, she was used to the erratic schedule of the ER where she worked. She thrived in the fast-paced environment and caught sleep where she could.

But for some reason she was feeling exhausted lately, especially since arriving here at the house.

It's stress. Between the death of her great-grandmother, learning that she owned a southern plantation house built in the 1800s, and the drive up to Natchez, she'd had a lot to deal with in three weeks. It was perfectly normal to feel stressed. After her great-grandfather, Jonathan had died last year, Arabella had taken a week off from work. Other than helping her great-grandmother with arrangements and things at home, Arabella had slept more than usual then too.

Sleep was a perfectly normal stress reaction.

Tomorrow. Tomorrow, she told herself, she would have ample time to sort through everything. The first thing on her list was to move some of the furniture back into a bedroom upstairs. Even though she was accustomed to catching sleep at the hospital in the break room they had set aside for physicians and other critical staff, but sleeping on a couch in the middle of this unusual chaos was definitely not her first choice.

And tomorrow she would determine what was going on in the world that required a handsome military officer to be here.

He's probably just part of the shared psychosis.

CHAPTER 10

*A*ugustus worked side by side with his men. After they dropped another tree, he took a moment to watch the sun coming up. Dawn was his favorite time of day. He liked watching the world ever so slowly wake up. Of course, since the war started, there was always the possibility that the day could bring destruction and death.

Augustus had more responsibility than he cared to think about. He was responsible not only for sending his men into battle, but also to mend them after they were wounded. The irony was not lost on him.

He'd been a soldier first, then barely out of medical school when the war started. He'd then been quickly promoted because he was one of the few doctors who was also an officer. It had gone well, until he'd been sent on this latest mission to Vicksburg. He was supposed to simply lead the men there, then hand them over to Pemberton and go back to practicing medicine. Such was the way of best laid plans.

A movement caught in the corner of his eyes had him turning his attention to the house. He shaded his eyes with a hand and squinted enough to see Arabella standing on the front steps. Her hands were on her hips as she gazed around. He watched as she went down the front steps of the house and walked around toward the back of the house. A couple of minutes later, she was back, still looking around as though she searched for something. What was she looking for?

She was wearing the same outfit he'd seen her wearing last evening – the denim trousers and undershirt. A black woman came out onto veranda and said something to her he couldn't make out. Arabella went back up the steps to follow the woman inside, but just before she went inside, she stopped and turned. Though it was hard to tell from this distance, Augustus was fairly certain her gaze was on his. He smiled.

She promptly turned and went back inside.

Augustus picked up a shovel and shook his head.

"Who was that?" Beau asked.

"I have no idea." Augustus didn't want the other men concerned with her.

"Maybe you should find out." Beau picked up his ax and split a log cleanly in two.

Yes. *My thoughts exactly.*

Augustus waited all of five minutes before he set off toward the house.

CHAPTER 11

*A*rabella followed a voluptuous black woman wearing a long costume to the kitchen. The woman muttered while they walked, not pausing for an answer.

"A lady ain't got no call to be walking around out there with all them soldiers running about. Them soldiers probably ain't seen no woman in months and most of 'em probly ain't ever seen a lady looks like you. Besides…" They had passed through the foyer and were heading into the back of the house. "you not wearing something you should be wearing. It just ain't fittin."

"Sit," the woman instructed when they reached the kitchen.

Arabella sat at a little table and watched the woman fill a plate with biscuits, bacon, and eggs and set it on the table in front of her.

"Eat." The woman nodded at the food. "It just ain't fittin. Them soldiers don't got no manners and they be getting the wrong idea. But don't nobody ever listen to Minny."

Deciding the woman's name must be Minny, Arabella broke off a bite of biscuit and tasted. Her usual breakfast, if she ate at all, usually consisted of a quickly grabbed carton of yogurt. Not that she was opposed to a hearty breakfast. Arabella just didn't like to waste calories on non-nutritional food that didn't even taste good.

The only person whose breakfast Arabella typically would eat was her great-grandmother's. Since no one else could cook the way her great-grandmother could, Arabella stuck with nutritional foods.

She broke off another bite and chewed.

This biscuit tasted unexpectedly like Vaughn's.

Arabella swallowed and stared at the plate in front of her.

Something was definitely odd.

This morning she couldn't find her overnight bag with her toothbrush, soap, and other toiletries. So she'd gone to her car to bring in her suitcase only to see no sign of her car. Stolen? Here, in the middle of nowhere?

In fact, there had been no modern vehicles in sight. Just horses and a wagon.

No cars. The costumes.

Perhaps they were filming a movie. It was a plausible explanation. Except for the fact that she was the owner and she hadn't given permission. *Maybe Vaughn gave permission before...*

There was still the mystery of how her car had gotten moved. Arabella couldn't find her handbag or her keys. She circled back around to her first thought that it had been stolen.

Absently, she picked up a slice of bacon and bit into it. She closed her eyes. Geez this was good. Bacon was something else she only ate on rare occasions. It was so damn unhealthy. Why were the good things in life always the things that were so bad?

Minny continued to talk. "And now we's stuck here with those men for who knows how long. So much for getting out of here and to safety of the town." She stopped long enough to raise a spoon in the air. "The good lord gonna have to look after us now."

Taking a deep breath and shutting off her racing thoughts while trying to ignore Minny's discourse, Arabella dug into the breakfast. The black woman glanced at her and grinned to herself as she continued to mumble. "I likes a lady with an appetite. Ladies always worrying about their waistline. Don't no man want no skinny girl. Haven't seen a lady with this good an appetite since…" Minny paused in mid-sentence, holding her spoon in one hand, the other hand on her hip, and stared at Arabella.

Arabella stopped eating long enough for a sip of water. She smiled at Minny. "This is good. Thank you." She hadn't realized she was hungry. But then working in the ER, she'd learned to ignore hunger cues.

Minny narrowed her eyes at Arabella and turned back to the stove. Thankful for the quietness, Arabella finished her breakfast in peace. Last night, someone, perhaps Minny herself, had warned her that they needed to leave. Now she'd just been told that they would be staying.

Not that Arabella planned to go anywhere anyway just yet. She wiped her hands on the cloth napkin and pulled her phone out of her pocket. Still no service. And only twenty-six percent battery left. She turned her phone off, something she never did, in order to conserve power.

Maybe there was a television around here. She needed to check the news. If anyone knew, Minny would. She appeared to have a pulse on things. "Do you have a TV?" Arabella glanced around the kitchen, but didn't see anything other than cookware and stacks of flour and potatoes.

Minny looked at her again, over her shoulder, eyes wide. Then turned her gaze back to the dough she was kneading. She mumbled to herself, but Arabella couldn't make out her words.

Perhaps a better idea was to find a landline and call the sheriff's department. At the very least, she needed to know what, if anything, was going on around here. Especially since she hadn't seen Jerry all morning. Maybe he was part of a scam and had just allowed her to assume he was the caretaker with permission to be here.

Deciding that searching for Jerry was the most logical first step in figuring out what was happening around here, Arabella left Minny and the kitchen behind to set off upstairs.

As she reached the stair landing, the clock chimed six times. The delicate chimes were soothing. She knocked on the first bedroom door on the left where Jerry had set up a sleeping area. When there was no answer, she knocked again and called his name. Still no answer.

She pushed the door open slowly and peeked inside the room.

Though she froze and her hand dropped from the knob, the door continued to swing open.

Arabella stared into the room, her mind blank with shock. This was the room where all the furniture had been stacked. The room where Jerry had a kept a bed for himself. There had been a little television next to the daybed.

Instead, the room was elegantly furnished with a four-poster bed standing in the center of the room. The bed was made with white linens and a pale pink blanket was folded across the foot of the bed. A bureau was on one side of the room and a vanity on the other. An open trunk sat at the foot of the bed. A little sitting area had been set up on the other side.

Arabella glanced over her shoulder, then stepped forward, drawn to the open trunk. She knelt in front of it and put her hands on the edges. There were what appeared to be infant clothing stacked on one side and a stack of papers on the other. The corner of a photograph caught her attention and she gently pulled it from the papers. It was actually a small piece of tin – what her great-grandmother called a tintype.

Arabella took the picture with her to stand at the window and held it up to the morning light.

The image was one of a young couple – a man and a woman – dressed in antebellum clothing. They both smiled, untypical for the period. An infant sat in the woman's lap.

Arabella squinted, pulling the image closer.

Her heart slammed against her chest and she grabbed hold of the drapes to steady herself.

The lady in the picture was Arabella.

CHAPTER 12

$\mathcal{A}$ugustus covered the distance in two seconds flat. The lady he'd admired from a distance was about to faint. He should know. With two younger sisters and their bevy of friends, he'd spent enough time with the female persuasion to have a decent sense of what fainting looked like. It was especially prevalent in the summer months with their tight corsets. They called it swooning and typically blamed it on whatever handsome man happened to be standing nearby.

Whatever they wanted to call it, the young lady was about to be passed out on the floor. Just as he reached her, she took two quick breaths. Putting one arm beneath her knees and the other beneath her shoulders, he swept her from her feet. She gasped.

As he carried her to the bed, he was aware that her arms were tight around his shoulders.

He'd reached her in time to prevent her from fainting. Relief rushed through him as he laid her on the bed and sat next to her.

"What are you doing?" Her eyes were wide open and focused on him.

"You were about to faint." She was even beautiful up close - her emerald eyes trimmed with thick black lashes and her kissable rose-colored lips. All framed by luscious smooth brunette hair.

"I most certainly was not."

"I'm a doctor. I can tell these things." There was a flush to her cheeks now and her eyes narrowed.

"In that case, perhaps you should return to medical school."

He stared at her a moment, then he laughed. "Perhaps you're right. Since obviously you didn't faint." He picked up a long strand of her soft hair and wrapped it around his finger.

"Who are you?" She pulled away, and he let the strand of hair drop. Her voice was soft, but laced with distrust.

Augustus stood up and bowed. "I apologize for my lack of manners. My name is Colonel Augustus Townsend." He stood up straight. "Or Doctor Townsend as the occasional may present."

She looked askance at him. "No. Really. Who are you?"

"Augustus Townsend." He said helplessly. "Of Jefferson County."

Her lips curved up at the corners. "Are you an officer or a doctor?"

"Both… Mostly a doctor."

She wrapped her arms around her knees. "Then you're a doctor in real life?"

Real life? When was life not real? "Of course."

She stared at him. He wondered what she was thinking. Her expression was calm, but probing as she watched him.

"May I be so bold as to ask your name?"

He didn't think she was going to answer at first. "Arabella," she said simply.

"Such a lovely name. It's a pleasure to meet you Miss Arabella." He held out his hand, palm up. When she put her hand in his, he bent and kissed the back of her hand.

She was holding something. "What do you have?"

"A picture." She glanced toward the photograph as though she had forgotten she was still holding it.

"May I see it?"

Again, she hesitated as though she weren't sure if she trusted him enough to share the picture. Yet she handed it to him. He took the photograph and held it toward the light. It was too dark to see. He nodded toward the window where she had been standing. "May I?"

"Sure."

Moving toward the light of the window, he studied the image. It was common enough – a man and a woman holding an infant in their arms.

Yet... He peered closely. The woman in the image was Arabella. He glanced toward her, still sitting on the bed. She was married, then, and had a child.

His heart sank. It was only to be expected. A woman as beautiful as Arabella would not go unwed. He went back to stand in front of her. "Again, my apologies, Madame. Is your husband a soldier in the war then?"

CHAPTER 13

Arabella sat in the middle of the bed, not daring to move. Colonel Doctor Augustus Townsend had been partially right. She had been about to faint. Fortunately, avoiding the quick decrease in blood pressure was second nature - sniff twice through her nose and gasp for air. The gasp had come natural enough when he'd swept her off her feet.

Arabella had a blood phobia, yet had made it through biology using that simple technique. She learned to inhale quickly and squeeze her fists to avoid falling out of her desk in the classroom. Fortunately, she'd only fainted in class once. The professor had kindly taken her aside and taught her how to avoid fainting. The technique had served her well through her internship allowing her graduate with honors.

Even though she hadn't fainted, there was still the problem of the picture. Arabella had not sat for that photograph. There must be someone who looked similar to her – a cousin perhaps. It explained the odd reaction she'd gotten from the elderly man as well as the woman who'd made breakfast for her. They'd simply mistaken her for the woman in the picture.

Though it didn't explain everything, Arabella had no other explanation at the moment.

The man knew my name.

The thought darted at the edge of her mind, but bounced away.

"That isn't me." She insisted.

She watched as a mixture of confusion and hopefulness crossed his features.

Then he turned the photograph over. And looked back at her with something akin to pity.

She held out her hand. When he placed the cool tintype in her hand, dread washed over her. She took her eyes from his and read the names written on the back of the picture. *Charles. Ericka. Arabella.*

Arabella pressed her fingers against her forehead. *No!* Her mother's name was Ericka and her father's name was Charles. They had died when Arabella was an infant.

Of course. They'd had this photograph taken before…

Exhaling, she looked down at the picture again. When she moved her thumb aside, she saw a date written in the corner. *1840.*

She handed the picture back to Doctor Colonel Augustus Townsend and rubbed her eyes with her palms. This was too much to think about. "Are you filming a movie?"

There was that look again. The one that she'd used so many times before. Most recently before she'd told a patient. *I think you need to go to the psychiatric hospital for a few days.*

He didn't answer. She glanced toward the window. Where were the trailers? The cameras?

Perhaps this was rehearsal. Or some type of immersion training to help get them into their parts. Sort of like learning French when the instructors only spoke French.

She looked back into his sky blue eyes. Tried to keep the

panic from her own eyes, but suspected that she failed miserably.

Something was not right. She just couldn't quite put her finger on it. It didn't help that the handsome doctor… officer was watching her. "I need to find Jerry." Since Jerry had been the last person who had made sense, it seemed like finding him was the best course of action at the moment.

"All right," Augustus agreed. "I'll help you."

He reached for her arm as she scooted off the bed. She jerked back. "I can do it."

He held his hands up, but stayed close to her. In fact, when her feet hit the floor, he stood only inches away. She stared at his broad chest and noticed for the first time that he was wearing the gray uniform of the Confederacy. She tilted her head up and gazed into those clear blue eyes.

He grinned at her and her stomach did a little summersault.

Until Arabella was about fifteen, her great-grandparents had taken her to museums and battlefields… Civil War reenactments. At fifteen, Arabella had begun choosing hanging out with friends to spending weekends with her family.

All those years spent watching reenactments and going to museums coalesced as she stared at Augustus.

Augustus was a Confederate soldier come to life.

Arabella swayed.

CHAPTER 14

ugustus had been right. Arabella had been going to faint. Unfortunately, he was a few minutes off on his diagnosis.

Now this elusive and beautiful woman was in his arms, her eyes closed, her body limp.

He gently laid her back on the bed, keeping her head up. "Arabella." He whispered her name. When she didn't answer, he squeezed her hand.

She blinked, then closed her eyes again. "You're safe Arabella."

She opened her eyes again and gazed into his. She was silent as the seconds ticked past. "You're real." Her voice sounded resigned. As though she had hoped he wasn't real.

"I'm very real." He held her hand tightly and swept the hair off her cheek. "How do you feel?"

"I've been better."

"It's been awhile since I had someone swoon at my feet." Actually he'd never had a woman swoon at his feet, but he wasn't about to tell her that. He was rather enjoying the moment.

"I didn't swoon." She scoffed. "I was just lightheaded for a minute."

His lips curved in amusement. "I'm a doctor. And I have two sisters. I know swooning when I see it."

"So you say." She went to sit up.

He put an arm around her shoulders to help. "There's no need to rush. You're safe here."

"I'm okay now." As though to prove her point, she slid off the bed and stood up.

CHAPTER 15

rabella took a deep breath. It had been quite some time since she'd passed out. She'd moved past her blood phobia by learning to focus. She was sometimes still caught off guard, but she knew how to inhale quickly twice and gasp. It sounded a little funny, but it worked.

But this time, there had been no blood. There had only been a solider standing in front of her. Standing directly in front of him, she'd realized just how tall he was – over a head taller than she and he stood tall and straight.

And now he was treating her as though she were fragile. *You're safe.* His words sent a rush of conflicting emotions through her. She felt petite standing so close to him. She also felt safe with his hand supporting her back. It was a reflex that had her jerking away.

Arabella was the strong one. The one who supported patients who were ill. Certainly not the other way around. Her eyes flicked to his face. He was watching her with genuine concern. He looked healthy. But then looks could be deceiving.

"You're wearing your uniform."

He glanced down as though noticing the uniform for the first time. A look of understanding crossed his features. "Your husband. He's a soldier then." It was more a statement than a question.

She hadn't answered him before when he'd asked about a husband. She squeezed her eyes tightly closed for a moment, feeling her brow furrowed between her eyes. She shook her head. "No." She opened her eyes and stared into his blue eyes, bright with concern.

"Jerry?"

Jerry. She thought of her fiancé, Matthew Caldwell Jennings, III. The man who wore a suit and tie to work everyday and never left the house in anything less than business casual – not even to dash to Starbucks to grab a morning latte. A bubble of laughter spilled from her lips. He tilted his head and the corners of his lips curved into the beginnings of a smile as he watched her.

"No."

"But he's a soldier?"

She tucked a strand of hair behind an ear. Shook her head.

"Then what-?"

Someone knocked on the side of the open door and his question was interrupted.

"Excuse me." Villars stood in the doorway, his arms loaded with material. "I'm sorry to interrupt."

Arabella answered quickly. "Please. Come in. You're not interrupting." Maybe a little, but she was thankful for the reprieve. The soldier's questions were getting a little too personal.

Villars took two steps before Augustus dashed over to take the load from his arms.

"Thank you, Sir. I find it hard to walk carrying things anymore."

"Think nothing of it." Augustus carried the load and dropped it onto the bed. "You brought gowns." He glanced at Arabella.

Villars stood next to them. "Yes. These are some of Mistress Erika's things. I believe they will fit Miss Arabella just right."

CHAPTER 16

rabella stared at the dresses on the bed. Gowns. There were two of them. Long dresses made from yards of chiffon. Ribbons and lace. All quintessentially feminine. One was light aqua, the other a silvery gray. The light aqua one was a ball gown and the gray one was a high necked day dress. Though she recognized the antebellum style from her museum days, these dresses were different. They were clean and well… new.

She turned and looked into Villars' eyes. Despite her insistence that the lot of them suffered from delusions, his eyes held something disturbing. As though he knew something important. Something that others would find disturbing.

Shaking off the fanciful emotions, she forced a smile on her face and reverted to what came natural. Years of training. "Thank you." Whatever his delusion, he believed it fervently and it wasn't her place to challenge those beliefs. "These were my mother's?"

"Yes ma'am. They are. Your mother couldn't take everything with her. There are others if these don't suit you."

Couldn't take everything? "Where did she go?"

Villars grinned broadly. "She's in New Orleans with Mister Brandon's wife. They left after we seceded." He scratched his chin. "That's been about two years ago. Maybe more."

Arabella looked questioning at Augustus. This man was babbling about her mother again. Her mother who had died when she was an infant.

Augustus watched her. "You didn't know. You don't remember your parents leaving, do you?"

It occurred to Arabella then that Villars may have known her parents. Perhaps they'd lived here, with her, before they had died. He thought they still lived.

Everything suddenly made sense. In the midst of a house full of people with delusions this man had dementia.

CHAPTER 17

ugustus watched Arabella carefully. If she were going to faint again, he wanted to be ready to catch her.

She watched both him and Villars with such distrust, Augustus was beginning to believe that she didn't know where she was. Besides swooning, she was disoriented. Perhaps she'd suffered a blow to the head.

"It's all right, Villars. I'll see that she's taken care of."

"I can take care of myself."

"Yes sir. Of course." He looked pointedly at Arabella. "If you need anything just pull the bell cord." He turned and, using his cane for support slowly made his way across the room toward the door.

Arabella turned and glared at him. Augustus swallowed a laugh. This woman who protested the fact that she swooned at the drop of a hat, had a fire to her that he found intriguing. "Do you know where you are?" He needed to assess her level of awareness.

"Of course."

He waited.

She scoffed. "I'm at my great-grandparents' house in Natchez."

"All right." He didn't doubt that the house had been in the family for generations.

"And your mother's name."

"Erika Becquerel. She died when I was an infant."

Augustus crossed his arms and sighed. This was where things became problematic. Again a basic assessment was in order. "What year is it?

"I'm oriented to place and time."

"Humor me."

She rolled her eyes.

"What can it hurt? Just tell me what year it is."

She stared into his eyes, her voice calm and sure. "2021."

CHAPTER 18

rabella put a hand on the bed, then jerked it back when she felt the chiffon beneath her fingers.

Augustus was distracting her. With his intense blue eyes were locked onto hers, she had trouble focusing on what he was asking her.

She'd given thousands of mental status exams. She could rattle off the questions in her sleep.

He obviously hadn't expected her to state the actual year. It was probably against the rules of whatever thing they had going to do so. But in her defense, he had asked. She didn't like being tested. And she refused to get caught up in their insanity.

Augustus reached over and swept a strand of hair off her face and peered into her eyes.

She snickered. "What are you doing?"

"Have you hit your head?"

"No." She didn't try to hide her indignation. Still she searched her memory. Had she hit her head. *No.* This man was trying to plant memories in her head. Very unethical. Or... maybe he hit his head. "What year do you think it is?"

His lips curved up at the corners and her heart stuttered.

She'd never been particularly attracted to men in uniform, so it wasn't that, but there was something about this guy.

"It's 1863." He didn't stutter. Didn't blink. Stayed in character.

She crossed her arms. She should have expected no less. These people were obviously professionals. Or totally convinced of their delusion. Turn about was fair play. "Ok. I know you can't answer me."

His brows furrowed, he watched her with skepticism on his face.

"I admire your devotion. But it's your turn to humor me. Just nod or shake your head." She lowered her voice to a whisper. "Are you part of a reenactment group?"

He gave his head one slow shake.

Okay. This was going to be difficult. "Are you in some type of immersion thing?"

Again, a slow shake, his eyes still on hers.

"Maybe in preparation for a reenactment?"

"No. Look." He glanced around. "I'm a doctor. We're in the middle of a war, so I couldn't take you to an asylum even if I wanted to."

A bubble of laughter spilled out before she could stop it. It was her job to hospitalize people. Not to be *hospitalized*.

"I think you should stay here and rest. Perhaps your memory will come back posthaste. I'll check back in on you after a bit."

Posthaste. The only other person she'd ever heard use that word was her great-grandmother. This was a bit surreal. Perhaps it wouldn't hurt to sit down a bit.

Augustus must have seen her sway because he reached out and put a hand on her elbow to steady her. She allowed him to lead her to a chair a few feet from the bed. Once she was seated, he knelt in front of her. He slid his hand from her elbow and held her hand lightly in his. "If you need anything, pull the bell cord." He nodded toward the strip of cloth hanging next to the bed. "Villars will send for me."

His touch was sending tingles along the nerves in her fingers. It was even more disconcerting that he wasn't affected. She tried to picture her fiancé, but her thoughts were too jumbled.

"Of course." Perhaps if she agreed, he would leave her and she could think again.

Instead, he tightened his grip on her fingers, lifted her hand to his lips, and kissed the back of her hand. His lips lightly brushed her skin, sending even more tingles all through her. Her heart beat dangerously as she lost herself in the pools of his deep blue eyes.

He laced his fingers with hers. The thought crossed through her mind that she should pull her hand away in protest. Instead, every nerve in her body was aware of him. He smelled of the outdoors and gunpowder.

The scent of gunpowder jarred her out of her trance. She pulled her hand from his, ignoring her body's protestations.

"I apologize, Miss Arabella." He stood up and towered over her. "Forgive me for being so forward."

She shook her head, no coherent words forming in her brain.

The situation had inexplicably gotten turned around. Somehow she had become the one who was out of place.

CHAPTER 19

Augustus bowed over Arabella's hand and quickly left her. His footsteps echoed on the hardwood floors as he retreated to his room. Standing in the center of the room, he noticed the sunlight streaming through the window.

He pressed a hand against the side of his head. He'd been on his way to pick up a map. Though he was close enough that the air smelled like home, he was unfamiliar with this part of Mississippi.

When he'd seen Arabella standing in the window, he'd forgotten all about his errand. His men would wonder what took him so long. A good officer worked alongside his men. He was a firm believer in that.

But Arabella had proven to be a distraction that he couldn't fight.

She was an enigma. She'd felt fragile as he'd held her in his arms – her body limp from fainting. But once awake, she'd exuded strength. Strength and resolve that he'd only seen in a few women – one of which was his mother. It wasn't anything she said. In fact, she seemed a little addled. Instead it was in the way she held herself. A confidence.

She'd been quiet as he kissed her hand, lost in her mystical green eyes. She'd seemed unaffected by his attention. Yet as he'd held her smaller hand in his, he'd fought the urge to pull her into his arms and taste her lips.

Unfortunately, he'd spent most of his time learning the art of medicine, not the art of courtship.

Perhaps he was insane himself to even think of courting a lady as disoriented as she. 2018. Where had she come up with such a date? He wanted to know more. To understand the inner world of her mind. And unlike his normal reaction, it wasn't just a doctor's curiosity.

Augustus wanted to know about Arabella as a person.

He wanted to feel his lips against hers.

The map. He was here to pick up the map.

Grabbing the map from the back of his bureau, he headed back outside. As he passed Arabella's room, he kept his eyes straight ahead.

He was here to fight a war. Not to fall in love.

CHAPTER 20

The moment Augustus walked out the bedroom door, Arabella sprang from the chair and dashed to pick up the photograph from the bed. She'd think about what happened with Augustus later. Right now, she had to make sense out of all these things that didn't add up.

The uniforms and costumes. Her missing car. No cell phone service. Villars knowing her name.

The photograph.

She turned the photograph over and read the words again. There was no mistaking the names or the date.

She studied the images on the front again. The girl holding the infant looked so much like Arabella. Maybe a few pounds heavier. Baby weight, Arabella surmised. She took the photo back to the window and looked more closely. It was a close up shot of the couple and their baby. There.

She squinted in the sunlight. The woman's hair was highlighted halfway down. She obviously had highlights that had grown out.

Arabella huffed out a breath, lowered the photograph to her side, and pushed aside the curtains.

The back yard was crawling with soldiers. When she'd circled the house earlier, she hadn't noticed, but here, on the second story of the house, she could see tent after tent, fires, and most of all, soldiers in ragtag uniforms.

Augustus had been well-dressed in his gray uniform. But these soldiers were in rags and some were even barefoot.

She jumped when a tree fell. Who had authorized cutting down her trees? She then saw the rows of trees stacked alongside each other. Soldiers sat with hatchets sharpening the ends.

It seemed a bit overkill for a reenactment. Someone could get hurt.

Surely, though, no one would be on the other side of this barricade.

This was one of those Civil War living history events. It had to be. She scanned the area for spectators, but perhaps it wasn't open to visitors yet.

Jerry should have said something to her about this. She would have been fine with it, of course, but it would have been nice to have been forewarned.

She sighed. Perhaps she'd been too quick to judge. Was that what Vaughn had been trying to tell her in the letter that had been ruined? She'd only been able to catch words here and there. *History. Antebellum. Family.*

When in Rome…

She went back to the bed and ran her fingers along the chiffon, examining the two dresses. One was obviously for formal occasions and the other appeared to be for everyday.

She picked up the everyday dress and opened the buttons. Fortunately, the buttons were on the front. Heavens, there must be twenty of them.

She slipped out of her jeans, pulled off her sweater, and slid the dress over her head. As she tugged it down, then began fastening the buttons, she was a bit stunned. The dress couldn't have fit better if it had been tailor-made for her.

Villars had said it belonged to her mother. No matter what was going on in his head, he was right about the fit.

She put her own boots back on, zipping them up.

Lifting the volume of skirt material to avoid stepping on it, she went to the free standing mirror in the corner and examined her appearance. The dress had a wide skirt, belling out – not a full hoop skirt, but wide nonetheless. Now she could fit in enough to determine what was going on.

She knew from her training and experience with clients that the most effective treatment technique was forming a therapeutic alliance – creating an environment of trust.

That's what she would do. She would appear to join in, find out what was going on and well… go from there. She certainly wasn't getting anywhere by questioning their beliefs.

She picked up a straw hat from the wardrobe, put it on top of her head, and tied the attached white ribbons into a bow on the side of her neck. Going back to the mirror, she adjusted the hat and managed to keep a straight face. Despite feeling ridiculous, she had only one thought.

What would Augustus think of her now?

CHAPTER 21

*A*ugustus climbed onto the makeshift parapet and looked toward the east. Even after they'd cleared a good-sized area, there were still too many trees to see the river.

Careful with his footing, he turned and looked back toward the plantation house. He tugged his hat down a bit to shade the heat of the noonday sun.

It had only been a few hours since he'd seen Arabella, but she was all he could think about. It didn't matter that she wore strange clothes and used odd language. It didn't even matter that she was addled.

She was the most enchanting woman he'd ever met. She was beautiful. And interesting.

He'd watched the house almost constantly, but he'd seen no sign of her.

Of course, he reminded himself, he'd told her to stay in her room and rest. Even as he'd made the suggestion, he strongly suspected Arabella was going to do whatever she wanted to no matter what he or anyone else said.

He smiled to himself as he climbed down and put both feet safely on the ground.

"Colonel Townsend." Beau called out to him.

Augustus hurried to where Beau and four other men were digging a trench. Granger, a young man not more than twenty, sat holding his ankle. His face contorted in pain.

Augustus slid into the trench next to Granger. "What happened?"

"I landed wrong."

"Let me see." He unlaced Granger's boot – what was left of the laces – and wiped the dirt from Granger's ankle. "Does this hurt?" He pressed against the side of his foot.

"No."

Augustus pressed on the other side. Granger inhaled sharply.

"Guess we found it."

"Is it broken?"

Augustus ran his hands along the boy's foot. "Nothing obvious. You might have a fracture. We need to get you inside the house. You're going to have to stay off of it." Augustus struggled to keep his voice steady. Another man down. They could only hope that they somehow managed to stay out of the path of the Yankees.

"How long?" Granger winced as Beau helped him stand.

The men, on the other hand, were itching to fight. "At least a week."

Granger groaned. "I can't be down Doc. I'm useless to you this way."

"You can still hold a rifle, can't you?"

"Yes sir." Granger straightened. "I can still aim for the blue bellies, too."

"You're good then. Let's get you inside to rest before the fighting starts." He and Beau began the walk to the house, Granger between them. "Don't put any weight on it."

Augustus lifted his eyes heavenward. *Please don't let the fighting come to our doorstep.*

CHAPTER 22

*A*rabella stood in front of the grandfather clock. She felt the key beneath her blouse and wrapped her fingers around it. The dress felt odd. Despite all the reenactments her grandparents had dragged her to, she'd never been expected to participate and it had never occurred to her to do so.

Someone had fixed the clock. She distinctly remembered a scar between the roman numerals six and seven. They'd cleaned it, too. The face that had looked faded was a little brighter now. They may have even replaced the face.

"It's a beautiful clock, isn't it?" Arabella jumped at the voice. She recognized the smooth voice as belonging to Augustus without even turning around.

"It has a large presence."

He moved around to stand next to the clock putting himself in her line of vision. "That's an interesting way to put it."

She shrugged and turned to look up at him. She was immediately reminded how tall he was. She could tell he'd been outside. He smelled of fresh dirt and pine needles with a hint of wood smoke.

The ticking of the clock echoed her heartbeat as she looked into his eyes. The corners of his lips curved into a smile as he reached out and straightened her hat.

Her lips parted and her cheeks flushed as a flurry of emotions rushed over her – a bit of embarrassment that she'd practically fainted in his arms earlier. And a bit of self-consciousness at the hat she'd impulsively tied on her head.

"You look…" He tilted his head to one side. "different."

She'd wondered how he'd react to her dress. Now she felt a little more ridiculous.

"I like it." He ran his hand lightly along her jaw, leaned in, and kissed her on the cheek.

Arabella stood still, not sure how to react. Her nerves were sending sparks through her body at the unexpected intimacy.

She completely forgot about how she was dressed and instead focused on him.

He smiled. "I wonder if you would do me a favor."

She attempted to focus on what he was saying. "Um." She blinked and focused on what he was saying. "A favor."

"Yes." He grinned.

"Sure." She looked back at him and returned his smile. What manner of trouble was this man determined to get her into? Already she'd put on a costume in order to blend in and gain his trust.

"One of my soldiers, Granger, fell into a hole and fractured his ankle. I need him to stay off his feet. Would you tend to him?"

Arabella cringed inwardly. *Tend someone?* Before she could form a response, he kept talking.

"His name is Granger and he's in the parlor."

"What does he need? I'm not that kind of doctor."

He scrunched his brow and tilted his head as though her words didn't compute. "Just bring him some water and whatever else he might need to keep him off his feet."

She crossed her arms and smiled sweetly. "Of course. I'd be happy to tend your wounded soldier."

The man obviously didn't understand sarcasm. "Thank you." He kissed her on the forehead. "I have to get back outside. We're a man down and there's a lot to do."

She rolled her eyes as he turned and darted out the front door.

Perhaps this blending in thing hadn't been such a good idea.

CHAPTER 23

The rain started at Noon and made the temperature bearable. Augustus was knee deep in mud when the courier brought news.

Out of the corner of his eye he saw the men gathering around and waiting for him to share the latest update on the war. As he listened to the emaciated young soldier who'd been given the dubious honor of riding at breakneck speed with news he had to keep in his head, his spirits sank.

Though the news was not unexpected, it was disheartening nonetheless. They were sitting right in the path of the Yankee soldiers marching to Vicksburg. Though there was a campaign by water up the Mississippi River, there was also a convergence of troops by land. And one was headed their way.

It was with a heavy heart that he turned to his men and gave them the news. News that sent them whooping with excitement.

CHAPTER 24

Arabella lifted her skirts enough that she didn't trip and went into the parlor. It would have been nice if they had at least left the air conditioning on. Even with the tall French doors thrown open, there was barely a breeze flowing through the house.

She cringed when she saw who must be Granger sitting in the parlor. His clothes were tattered and he was covered in dirt, his bare feet resting on the sofa. He was young and his face was scrunched in obvious pain.

This man needed pain medication. Surely the rules could be broken when someone was injured.

He looked up and his face brightened with hope when he saw her. Any resentment she'd been feeling at being asked to look after him dissipated. "Are you Granger?" When he nodded she continued. "I'm Arabella."

"You're an angel."

She chuckled. "No. But I might can help some with the pain. Have they given you any medication?"

He shook his head.

"Nothing?"

"No ma'am."

"Not even Tylenol?"

He wore a similar expression that Augustus had worn earlier. As though she were speaking a language they didn't understand.

"Never mind. Can I sit with you for a moment?"

"I'd be honored." He pulled his legs up, favoring his ankle.

Thankfully, there was no blood. "I'll just sit over here in the chair."

He nodded and stretched his leg back out. "I apologize, Miss, for not standing up."

She perched on the edge of the chair, careful to keep her skirts down. "No need to apologize. Tell me what happened."

CHAPTER 25

The rain had moved out, leaving Augustus and his men soaked. As the rain moved out, the sun returned with a vengeance. Though their clothes dried quickly, they were miserably hot. Augustus felt like he was baking in his uniform. His men seemed to be fairing no better if the sweat rolling down their faces was any indication.

He stood on the parapet trying to decide if they had time to lodge another line of defense. They had trees… they had a trench… He was a doctor first and had never been more aware of that fact than at this moment.

My kingdom for a cannon.

His gaze followed his thoughts toward the house – as they had done a hundred times that day.

What was Arabella doing now?

He tried to ignore the unfounded jealousy he felt toward Granger at getting to spend the day with her.

Would she read to him? Perhaps write a letter for him? It didn't matter what they did. Even if they did nothing but be in the same room together, Augustus envied the man.

Augustus had never been so enamored of a lady before. What spell had she woven over him?

He smiled to himself. Whatever it was, he liked it. This heady feeling was nothing he'd experienced before.

"Sir."

Augustus turned to see Beau pointing toward the tree line.

Pointing toward what looked like a row of blue bellies.

CHAPTER 26

*A*rabella stared out the front window as everyone ran around her.

"Get down!"

"It's the Yankees!"

"Load the guns."

It was too far from the river here, so anyone coming in would have be on foot or on horseback… Or car, of course.

Still. No filming crew. Despite what Augustus said, it had to be one of those realistic reenactments. The ones where people participated just for the experience. No audience.

They called themselves living historians engaged in total immersion events. No audience needed. Jonathan, her grandfather, had gone to a few of these. He called it *experimental archaeology.* If she remembered correctly, he had gone to one a few years ago at Vicksburg for the days leading up to the fourth of July. He'd been thrilled with the experience – except of course for the blistering July heat. Arabella never quite understood her grandparents' fascination with antebellum and Civil War history. It was just their thing.

There was really no other explanation. She needed to find her car. It seems she hadn't chosen the best time to show up here. It was still baffling why Jerry hadn't said anything to her about it. It was even more confusing why she couldn't locate him.

"They're coming." Someone yelled.

As everyone scrambled around her, Arabella watched as a wall of soldiers in blue approached. They first appeared at the road, then spread out, melding along the tree line. Even knowing they weren't a real danger, her heart rate tripped up a notch and she couldn't take her eyes off of them.

Suddenly everything in the house was quiet. She glanced around at the dozen or so people around her, crouched behind the sofa, a tipped over dining table, stack of cotton bales.

Cotton bales? In the house? When had they brought those inside?

"Miss." A man called out to her. "Miss, you best take cover."

"Right." She turned and went to sit on the bottom step of the staircase. This must be the moment they'd all been planning for. It would be interesting to watch this play out.

She gasped at the sound of a cannon ball coming toward them. She recognized it as a cannon ball from the reenactments she'd attended.

Someone screamed.

Though it landed just outside the walls, the crash shook the whole house. Arabella instinctively covered her face with her arms. Bits of debris flew everywhere.

Then the bullets started coming. Arabella stood up and dashed toward the first thing she could find.

The grandfather clock. Using both hands, she shoved it out a foot from the wall – just enough so that she could fit behind it. Its slow steady ticking belied the obvious danger of the situation.

This was a little too realistic for her.

She placed her cheek against the cool wood of the clock and closed her eyes. *Something must have gone wrong.* Even in reenactments and training exercises, people could get hurt.

Her eyes flew open when someone screamed only a few feet away. A young boy, not more than ten, stumbled on the stairs. Blood gushed from his leg.

She put both hands against the back of the clock and fought the urge to run help him. But she knew better than to put herself in danger. *You have to protect yourself if you're going to help others.* Part of the intensive training from the ER. She inhaled deeply three times. There would be time to help him when the shooting stopped. She knelt behind the clock to make herself a smaller target. Just in case.

She focused on the steady ticking of the clock while pushing the sounds of gunfire to the back of her mind. Another cannon ball came toward them. She held her breath, but it landed somewhere else.

In the aftermath of the high pitched cannon ball, she heard what sounded like a Comanche tribe on the warpath outside. The ringing in her ears and the yelling couldn't disguise the sound of more bullets. She glanced toward the young black man sitting on the stairs.

Real bullets. They were using real bullets. There had to be a law against this sort of thing. But for right now, she would stay put. *Take care of yourself first.*

She closed her eyes and waited. A door slammed from the back of the house, but all their attention was trained on the front. She wanted to scream at them. *Watch your back. The enemy has you flanked.*

She was frozen between skepticism that this was real and what she was seeing with her own eyes – an injured child, bullets flying amidst cannon fire, and what she knew of battle tactics.

Her grandparents did this to her. *Too many history lessons, museums, and tale of days gone by.*

She felt the clock shudder the same time she felt something graze her cheek. She put her fingers against the sting, then brought her hand down and stared at the blood on her fingers.

CHAPTER 27

*A*ugustus watched as the cannon ball crashed against the front of the house, spewing mud and debris everywhere. There were a number of people inside. But he couldn't think about anyone other than Arabella.

He had to get inside. But right now, if he set off across the field, he would be either shot or hit by a cannon ball.

He glanced around at his men. Their clothes may be ragged, but they were strong. They could take down a handful of Yankees.

August held up his rifle. "Charge!" He yelled the word and his men set off across the field with the rebel yell that had been known to freeze the blood of Yankee soldiers. To Augustus, it sounded more like a pack of wild dogs charging across the fields.

As his men raced toward the enemy soldiers, Augustus raced toward the back of the house and crashed through the back door, slamming it against the wall. "Don't shoot," he called out. "It's me. Doc Townsend."

When he reached the foyer, there were four guns trained on

him. Four guns that were quickly lowered when they saw that he was who he said.

"Anyone hurt?" He asked automatically, all the while, his eyes scanning for Arabella.

"Jeremy got hit in the leg."

"No one else got hit."

"Good." Augustus walked through the debris from the cannon fire and swept aside the tattered portieres and watched as his men chased the enemy soldiers using a mixture of their sharpshooting and the eerie sound of their rebel yell.

Confident that they were safe for the moment, he turned back toward the room. Scanned unsuccessfully for Arabella. "Has anyone seen Miss Arabella?"

No answer. A couple of women glanced at him, shook their heads, and focused back on the front of the house. Augustus walked toward the injured boy on the stairs. As he neared him, the boy pointed toward the grandfather clock.

Augustus turned, noticing first that the clock was silent.

Then he saw Arabella, her face smeared with blood.

CHAPTER 28

*A*rabella had never been so glad to see someone as she was to see Augustus coming toward her.

After a cursory examination of her face, he pulled her to him in a hug. Tucking her head beneath his chin, he cupped the back of her head, holding her close as she trembled in his arms. "This is too real," she murmured.

"Much too real." His voice was soft against her ear.

"It's not a reenactment."

There was more gunfire in the distance. A dog barked somewhere outside. "No." He shifted to study her face again. "You're hurt."

She shook her head. "It's just a scratch."

"It's bleeding. Let me clean you up."

"The boy." She turned her gaze toward the stairway. "Help him."

"You'll stay here for a few minutes?"

She nodded.

"I'll come back for you."

After he left her to tend the boy, Arabella took stock of her injuries. He'd been right. She was bleeding. Fortunately, the sight of her own blood no longer bothered her. She lifted the hem of her skirt to wipe the blood from her cheek, then wiped the blood from her hands.

She could no longer hear the gunfire and the people in the house were moving about now, cleaning up.

Arabella walked around to the front of the clock that had saved her life, her boots crunching on bits of glass on the floor. The glass came from the shattered front door of the clock. She pressed her fingers against the clock's face.

Against the jagged rip between the numerals six and seven.

The rip that had not been there earlier in the day.

The rip that had been there when she first saw the clock.

She gripped the edge of the clock, then slid her hand down the cool wood as she dropped to the floor.

This was no reenactment. No Folie a deux.

This was real. Much too real.

CHAPTER 29

*A*ugustus checked the boy's leg. He was going to be all right. The bullet had merely grazed him and lodged itself in the wall. He would bandage the boy up, insist he get bed rest, and get back to Arabella.

He found her sitting in a chair talking with Granger. He held back, listening. He'd expected Granger to be comforting her, but instead, he found the opposite.

"Please tell me you're joking." Arabella's expression was a mixture of shock and skepticism. "I've never heard of anyone having sixteen siblings."

Granger laughed. "Yes ma'am. There are seventeen of us."

"Surely you must have different mothers."

"Nope." Granger appeared to be enjoying the attention a little too much. "My mother gave birth to all seventeen of us right there in her bedroom. We all have the same father, too."

Arabella hid a smile behind her hand. "Where do you all sleep?"

"Us boys, we sleep in the barn. There's nine of us. The eight girls, well… they sleep in the attic."

"My goodness. Your parents have a lot of mouths to feed."

"We grow our own food." Granger's face sobered. "But since the war, I fear for the women-folk."

"I can only imagine it must be difficult to be so far away from your loved ones."

Granger wiped at his nose and turned his head away. "I'm worried about my little sisters and my mother."

"You feel helpless being so far away from them."

Granger's shoulders shook.

Granger was crying? It was a rare thing to see a soldier cry. He'd seen soldiers have bullet wounds removed – with no chloroform – and never make a whimper. His soldiers needed to be strong and to show no signs of weakness.

He chose the moment of silence to step forward, clearing his throat. "Miss Arabella. I should tend to your wound now."

"Oh." She wiped at her cheek. "I'd forgotten about it."

Granger swiped his face on his sleeve and lifted his head, shifting to sit up straight. Other than a bit of redness around his eyes, any sign of weakness was gone.

"How's the ankle?"

"Good, Sir. I'm ready for duty whenever you say."

"Stay off of it." Augustus knelt next to Arabella and ran a thumb over her cheek. "Does it hurt?"

She shook her head.

Augustus stopped a young black woman on her way by. "Would you get a basin with some hot water? And a cloth?"

"Of course, Sir." The girl dashed off.

"You were very lucky."

"I don't feel very lucky right now."

"Did you fall?" Augustus took her hands and turned them palms up, examined them. "When the bullet hit?"

"No. It felt more like a bee sting than anything else."

The girl returned with a basin of water. Augustus squeezed

the water from the cloth and gently wiped away the already dried blood on her cheek.

"I must look a sight," Arabella commented, seeing the water turn red when he cleansed the cloth and started over.

"You look beautiful."

Arabella smiled. Charming, chivalrous men of the… south.

CHAPTER 30

For a woman who denied any propensity for swooning, Arabella fainted more than any woman he'd ever met. And that included all his sisters' silly friends, who swooned whenever a handsome man came near them.

Arabella did not seem like that swooning type and surely she didn't find him so handsome as to feign swooning for his attention. No. She wasn't that type either.

Yet she'd passed out in his arms.

Again.

Granger was on his feet and at their side less than a second after it happened. "Can I help?"

"No." Augustus snapped. "But I need your couch."

"Of course." Granger limped aside and made room for Augustus to pass, his arms full of woman and skirts.

He settled her on the sofa and gently patted her cheeks. "Arabella. Arabella. Wake up." He untied the ribbon from beneath her chin and removed her hat. She blinked and looked around, confused.

"What happened?"

"You fainted." He tossed the hat onto the nearest chair.

She put her hands over her face, glanced at Granger, who was hovering at her feet, then turned her green eyes to his. "It's the heat."

Augustus didn't doubt that the heat had been the cause of her fainting. "You're wearing too many clothes."

"I know." She readily agreed.

Augustus had expected her to disagree. To point out the impropriety of the remark. Instead, she leaned toward him. "Can I talk to you in private?"

"Of course." Without looking at him, Augustus told Granger to go outside.

"But, Sir. You told me to stay off my feet."

"Yes, well." He looked at the soldier who couldn't take his eyes off Arabella. "Go outside and put your feet up."

"Yes sir." Granger stood up and limped toward the front door.

"We could have moved." Arabella suggested.

Augustus shrugged. "It's easier if he goes."

"He needs a bath."

Augustus waited a beat, then when her words sank in, he burst into laughter. "I agree. We all need a bath."

"He's worse."

Augustus wasn't sure if that was a way of her telling him that he, too, needed a bath, but if it was, he couldn't disagree. "Is that why you wanted to speak to me privately? To tell me that we all need baths?"

She smiled then.

She smiled and his heart went into a dangerously fast pace. He'd already thought her beautiful, but when she smiled, her face lit up and her already unsurpassed beauty increased tenfold.

"I need you to speak truthfully to me."

"I've never spoken anything other than the truth to you."

She narrowed her eyes at him, but continued. "I need you to

take away all the reenactments or… unusual beliefs and speak frankly with me. As truthfully as you would if we met on the street in New York."

Augustus didn't see what New York had to do with anything, but he would have told Arabella anything. "You have my word."

"And your word is good?"

"Of course. May I?" He indicated the edge of the couch.

She moved aside and allowed him to perch on the edge of the couch next to her.

"You mustn't tell anyone about our conversation."

"Again. You have my word."

She nodded then glanced around. The room had emptied but she kept her voice at a whisper nonetheless. "What year is this?"

"1863."

She nodded slowly. "And you'd tell me that even if we weren't here. If we were somewhere else? Someplace normal?"

He shrugged. What did she mean by normal? "I don't think the year would change no matter where we found ourselves."

She took a deep breath. She told him earlier that it was 2018. Was she still harboring that belief?

"For me, the year has changed."

Augustus braced himself.

CHAPTER 31

Arabella knew in her heart that she had somehow stepped into another time.

Everything was different. The air felt different. It was quiet. She hadn't heard an airplane or a vehicle or anything even remotely tied to her life since since she'd awoke on this couch.

She was in 1863.

Right in the middle of the Civil War.

Her first impulse had been to tell Augustus. To convince him that she was from the future.

But as she looked at him, his expression one of innocent expectation, she couldn't do it. She couldn't shatter his belief that she was simply a southerner just like him trying to make it through to the end of the war. The war that was destined to go on for another two long years. A war that would be fought for naught. A war that would be all but forgotten in one hundred fifty years.

"It's nothing." She smiled. "A mere flight of fancy."

"You don't seem prone."

He was unexpectedly perceptive. And he was right. She wasn't prone. "It's the heat."

He seemed to consider the possibility. "It could be. And…" He nodded toward her voluminous skirts. "You're wearing a lot more clothes than you were this morning."

Picturing her jeans and tee-shirt, she felt her skin flushing. *I won't faint again. I will not faint again in front of this man.*

"I'm not sure which outfit I like better." There was a teasing tone to his voice. "Although this one is more feminine, the other revealed more feminine curves."

She chuckled. "I don't think you're supposed to say that."

"I know I'm not. But you know it's true."

She shrugged. "What are you going to do now?"

"What do you mean?"

"Now that your men have run off the Yankees." She said the words as matter of factly as she could even though they sounded strange to her own ears.

"We'll regroup." He didn't seem to find anything strange about their conversation. "Then we'll continue on as we had planned."

"And what is it that you had planned?"

"We'll proceed to Vicksburg."

Vicksburg. 1863. "No," she uttered.

"We must. General Pemberton has requested our help."

She put a hand on his. "Augustus." She looked deep into his blue eyes. "Don't do it. Don't go to Vicksburg."

"Why not?"

CHAPTER 32

"*S*ir. A messenger brought you a letter."

Augustus was forced to turn his attention from Arabella. Another messenger. This couldn't be a good sign.

A young black man he didn't recall seeing before stepped forward when Augustus stood and turned toward him. "Is he still here?"

"No sir. He was on his way to the post in Vicksburg." The man peeked around Augustus at Arabella.

Augustus shifted to block his view as he held out his hand. The boy stepped forward and placed the letter in his hand.

"Thank you."

"My pleasure, Sir."

Augustus took the letter and sat in the chair that Granger had vacated. Arabella silently watched him.

Augustus opened the letter with great trepidation in his heart.

Dear Augustus,

It is with a heavy heart that I write this letter to you as I know that you were stout friends during the Battle of Manassas. Thomas

Jackson was mistakenly shot by his own men on May 2, 1863 and subsequently died eight days later on May 10, 1863.

Augustus stopped reading and let his hand clutching the paper, drop to his side.

"Have you received bad news?" Arabella's voice jarred him out of his shock.

"Yes."

"Your family?"

"No." Augustus shook his head. "A dear friend." He looked into her eyes. "Another good man lost in battle."

"Too many."

"Yes. Too many."

"I'm sorry."

"Thank you."

"Do you want to talk about it?"

"No." Augustus leaned back in the chair and closed his eyes. "He was one of the best."

"What was his name?"

"Jackson."

He heard her quiet gasp. "Stonewall Jackson."

He opened his eyes and looked at her. "Yes. How did you know?"

She hesitated. "Everyone knows him."

CHAPTER 33

*A*rabella took a deep breath. She knew too much. And none of it was good. Still. It would do no good to panic.

History was unfolding before her eyes, but there was nothing she could do to change it. It flowed like a river. Taking its course where it would. Any influence she might attempt would merely be washed away like grains of sand and carried along with the flow.

"You knew him?" She stepped into her role as psychologist like stepping into her favorite pair of sweatpants after a long day at work. It came naturally without thought.

Yet he was talking about Stonewall Jackson. One of the most famous men in American history. She wouldn't have been an all-American southern girl if she hadn't had a hitch in her reaction.

"Yes. We fought together at Manassas."

"The Battle of Bull Run." She was stalling, trying to get her bearings. "That was a couple of years ago, right?"

"That's correct."

He rubbed at his eyes and she felt a need to go to him. To

comfort him. How many people had she walked through a crisis?

Unable to sort out why this felt different, she sat and quietly waited for him to say more.

"He always managed to have fresh fruit with him."

"Fruit?" It would normally be an odd thing to remember about someone, but maybe not so much in the 1800's.

"Yes. His favorite was lemons."

She nodded. Allowed him time to process. Lemons. Not something that was in the history books. "Can I help?"

He turned and looked into her eyes. "Yes."

CHAPTER 34

ugustus almost laughed out loud as he watched Arabella's eyes widen. He wondered what thoughts were going on in her head.

Other than her eyes, she showed little expression.

He held out the letter to her. "Would you read this letter out loud to me?" He told himself that it was too painful to read himself, but he knew that he really just wanted to hear her voice.

She took the letter and studied it.

"You can read? I assumed." He felt a surge of panic. If she couldn't read, then he'd just put her in an awkward position.

Glancing up at him beneath thick black lashes, she smiled. "The handwriting is difficult."

"If you can't read, I can read it myself. He held out a hand for the letter, but she ignored him. Instead, she started to read aloud.

Dear Augustus,

It is with a heavy heart that I write this letter to you as I know that you were stout friends during the Battle of Manassas. Thomas Jackson was mistakenly shot by his own men on May 2, 1863 and subsequently died eight days later on May 10, 1863.

A bullet shattered his left arm and it had to be amputated. Pneumonia soon set in and he began to fade. I regret that you weren't there. Perhaps he would have fared better. Though he lost his right arm, I lost my right hand.

We must expect reverses, even defeats. They are sent to teach us wisdom and prudence, to call forth greater energies, and to prevent our falling into great disasters.

Be wary my friend. And be safe.

I thought you might want to know his last words. He said "Let us cross over the river and rest under the shade of the trees."

WITH GREAT SADNESS.
Yours truly,
--Robert E. Lee

ARABELLA'S VOICE FADED AS SHE READ THE SIGNATURE. SHE spoke Robert E. Lee's name reverently. When she raised her eyes, they were filled with unshed tears.

Augustus allowed the pain of the loss of his friend to wash over him. It somehow seemed bearable with Arabella at his side.

She had a calming presence unlike any he had ever encountered in a female.

"You know Robert E. Lee?"

He nodded. "Our families have been friends for years. We only encountered each other a couple of times socially due to distance, but we spoke at length a few months ago."

She carefully refolded the letter and handed it back to him. "I'm so sorry for your loss."

The thickness in his throat returned and he looked away. He would grieve for his friend. Later. In his own way.

Right now he needed to track down his soldiers.

CHAPTER 35

As Arabella watched Augustus walk away from her, she absorbed his sadness, put it in the little compartment that she reserved for patients, and squared her shoulders.

What was she supposed to do now?

Granger limped back inside and she sighed. She was to nursemaid Granger. He grinned at her.

She stood up, moved away, and gestured to the sofa. "You're supposed to have your foot elevated."

"I did." He insisted.

She pointed at the couch. "Sit." She knew that look on his face and it so wasn't going to happen. "I'll be back after a bit to check on you." With that, she went out back, found a rocker on the back veranda, and created her own little breeze.

Now that she was alone, she could think.

Robert E. Lee and Stonewall Jackson. Augustus personally knew both of them. That thought alone was overwhelming.

The other overwhelming realization was that she was here in 1863. Was this what her great-grandmother was keeping from her? Was there a portal here that sent people back in time? If so what triggered it?

Her analytical brain wanted to know. To figure it out.

She caught her breath on her next thought.

Was it possible that her parents were still alive?

CHAPTER 36

*A*ugustus had need to get away. Just hearing Arabella reading aloud the words of his dear friend Robert E. Lee informing him that another of his dear friends had been killed – by his own men, no less, had been heartbreaking.

General Lee had intimated that perhaps Augustus could have done more to save their mutual friend, but Augustus knew that wasn't likely. Conditions on and around the battlefield were limited at least and abhorrent most of the time.

He sucked in a deep breath. This would pass. It was the way of war.

Augustus stood on the back veranda watching as his men came straggling back. He waited until he saw Beau coming forward, supporting another soldier who was limping to join them. He knew better than to ask who won.

"How did you fare?" He took the man's weight, giving Beau a break.

"I'm not sure. They retreated into the trees. I had to call the men back."

"We'll set up an infirmary on the bottom floor of the house."

Augustus and Beau got the man up the back steps and inside the house.

Beau winced as drops of blood splattered on the wood floor. The house would never be the same. He pictured his own home in Jefferson County and as always wondered how it and his family fared. "Get something and get this blood up."

He and Beau set the man on the floor of the study. "And gather up all the blankets you can find."

Augustus examined the man's leg. The bullet was still there firmly lodged in his calf. He was going to have to get it out. "You're Tom, right?"

The boy, not more than seventeen nodded, his cheeks streaked with tears that had fallen through the dirt on his face.

"I'm going to have to get this bullet out."

"Yes sir."

"I have to leave you while I get my instruments."

Augustus had some chloroform in his bag upstairs. As he rounded the corner, he couldn't help but glance toward the parlor for a glimpse of Arabella. He saw Granger on the sofa, but no sign of her. He took the stairs two at a time and grabbed his bag where he'd left it sitting next to the nightstand.

As he went back into the hallway, Villars stopped him. "Excuse me, Sir?"

Augustus stopped.

"They said you be needing some blankets and such."

"That's right. Do you mind?"

"Oh no sir. I just wanted to ask if there's anything else you'll be needing to help treat the wounded soldiers."

"As a matter of fact, there are a few other things that you might be helpful if you have them."

It was several minutes later when Augustus made it back downstairs. The first thing he noticed when he entered the study was the stack of blankets several feet high stacked against the wall.

The second thing he noticed was Arabella kneeling next to Tom, holding his hand. Tom no longer had tears in his eyes. He was talking about his family.

"My Pa didn't go to war. He's older – thirty-five. He stayed back to take care of my mother and the farm."

"Do you have any brothers?"

"No ma'am. I'm the only child. My ma, she took it pretty hard when I left."

"I can only imagine that she must be very proud of you."

Tom smiled.

Augustus walked up to the other side of Tom. He sent up a silent prayer that Tom was one of the lucky ones who got to go home whole after being shot.

CHAPTER 37

When Arabella looked up at Augustus, she saw the regret in his eyes as he watched Tom. The boy's wound must be worse than it looked.

Then Augustus shifted his gaze to hers and she caught her breath at the way he looked at her. His eyes softened and his lips curved slightly at the edges. "Thank you," he mouthed.

She nodded slightly, but turned her gaze back to Tom. "The doctor's here now. He's going to take a look at that wound."

Tom's expression turned to one of panic. "Will you stay?" His eyes widened. "Please?"

Arabella looked up at Augustus. He shrugged. "All right. I'll stay."

Arabella had made sure to sit facing away from Tom's gunshot wound. The last thing she needed was another fainting incident.

"Tell me about your farm." She urged as Augustus knelt and began examining the boy's wound.

Tom talked about his horse named Cherry. Arabella focused on his words to keep from focusing on the sound of Augustus ripping his pants.

Tom was still talking when he passed out.

"I think he fainted."

"Good." Augustus opened his medical bag. "We need to conserve all the morphine we can."

Arabella kept her gaze on Tom's face. "How bad is it?"

"It's not so bad right now, but if it gets infected, we'll have to take his leg."

Take his leg. "You mean you'll have to amputate?"

"It's the only way to keep the infection from spreading."

Arabella closed her eyes. She was quite familiar with the problem of infection during this time period. She was also aware of the tendency of physicians to amputate a limb to keep the infection from spreading. "I hope you can avoid having to do that."

"You know." Augustus said. "I'm not sure you should be here while I do this."

"Why not?"

"I don't need you fainting again."

"Don't worry. I'm not looking."

He didn't answer for a few minutes. "Got it."

"That was fast."

"Unfortunately, I've become an expert at digging bullets out of flesh."

"A dubious honor."

He scoffed. "No truer words were ever spoken."

Suddenly Arabella needed some fresh air. The smell of blood permeated the room. "Will you help me stand?"

"Of course." Augustus wiped his hands, then reached under her arms and lifted her off the floor.

With her feet on the floor, she put a hand on the arm he offered to steady herself. She felt the muscles under his sleeve. "Thank you."

"My pleasure. May I walk you to the back veranda?"

She nodded. Her pulse had quickened and she didn't trust

herself to answer. They were halfway to the door when she stopped. "What about Tom? We can't just leave him."

"He'll be fine."

"What if he wakes up?"

"I'll come right back."

He was right, of course. This wasn't the ER where she worked with plenty of staff to stay with patients and monitor them as needed. She would come back and check on him after she'd settled her stomach.

Augustus opened the back door, stepped aside to give her space to move her skirt through the door, and followed her out onto the veranda.

She expected to see a few of his men gathering around, take stock of the skirmish. Instead, she saw something quite unexpected.

The lawn was crawling with wounded soldiers.

CHAPTER 38

ugustus spotted Beau who was talking to another officer he didn't recognize.

"Please excuse me." Augustus turned to Arabella, took her hand and brushed the back with his lips. "Duty calls."

"Of course."

Though Augustus didn't want to leave her side, he had wounded to tend. Besides, he needed to find out where all these soldiers came from.

"Sir." Beau came toward him, bringing the other officer with him. "We met up with another regiment out there. This is Captain Jones. He's from the 22nd Louisiana detachment. They're on their way to Vicksburg, too, but they got waylaid by the same Yankees that got us.

Augustus shook hands with Captain Jones. "Welcome. Do you have a physician on staff?"

"We did and he was a fine good one, but we lost him at Port Hudson." Captain Jones took off his cap and lowered his head for a moment.

"I'm sorry to hear that." Augustus particularly didn't like it that physicians were in danger during battle – for a number of reasons, some admittedly personal.

Beau jumped in. "Colonel Townsend is our physician."

Augustus knew perfectly well why Beau was making sure he was known as the physician. He was preserving his claim as the captain in command. "I'll do what I can, but I'll need to request the assistance of anyone who has experience with the treatment of wounds."

Before getting to work, Augustus glanced toward the now empty back veranda. Arabella must have gone back inside. He would have been inclined to ask for her help, but there was a strong likelihood that she would faint at the sight of blood.

It was going to be a long day.

CHAPTER 39

Arabella went inside, woke up Granger, and moved him to the study with Tom. She thought he over-exaggerated his limp so she didn't offer assistance. Once he was situated, she located a pile of clean sheets, and set up a work station on the desk in the study. This way she could keep an eye on the patients while she worked.

Using a letter opener she found in the top desk drawer, she began ripping the sheets into long strips. When she had a foot or so of them ready, she gathered them up and headed out back. It looked like Doctor Colonel Augustus Townsend was going to be needing them for bandages.

"Excuse me." She stopped the first solider that passed by. "Have you seen the doctor?"

The man pointed toward a tent. "Thank you." She gathered up her skirts with her other hand and, ignoring the curious stares of the other soldiers, and several offers to carry the stack of bandages for her, picked her way to Augustus.

His back was to her, but she recognized him immediately by the broadness of his shoulders and the way his dark hair brushed his collar. She also recognized his voice when he told the solider "This might hurt a little."

She stood waiting until he finished stitching up the man's forehead. She was careful to fix her gaze on the trees on the horizon, though in all truthfulness, needles didn't bother her.

He turned and she saw a mixture of surprise and pleasure on his face.

"I brought you something." She held out the bandages for him to take.

"Where did you get these?"

"I made them," she said proudly.

"How did you know?"

She shrugged. "It wasn't hard to figure out. You've got a yard full of injured soldiers."

"Here." He pulled a stool forward. "Have a seat."

"Oh no. I'm good. Sitting is the new smok-" She promptly sat on the stool.

He looked askance at her, but tossed the bandages over his shoulder. He turned back to the man whose stitches he'd just finished.

Arabella followed his gaze. The man was grinning like an idiot.

She adjusted her hat and smiled back at him.

"You can go now," Augustus said.

The man jumped off the stool he'd been sitting on and dashed away.

Augustus propped his foot on the stool and studied her. She shifted uncomfortably on her own stool.

"How would you like to be of use?"

I just brought you bandages that I made myself. Clean ones. She didn't have time to formulate an answer before he continued. "I know you have an… aversion to the sight of blood, but I think I have the perfect job for you."

"Okay."

"I'd like you to provide morale for the soldiers."

"Morale? What do you mean?" Her brain went to cognitive behavioral therapy. Perhaps her training in psychology would come in use after all. It was something she hadn't considered.

"Just sit there and smile at the men."

"Smile at them? That doesn't sound very useful. I could talk to them though."

"You can talk if you want to, but mostly just sit there and look pretty."

A laugh escaped before she could stifle it. He must be insane. *He wants me to be Scarlett O'Hara.*

CHAPTER 40

*A*ugustus laughed to himself at her expression of disbelief.

"I can do other things, you know."

"I'm not discounting that. But right now these men." He gestured around him at the men in the yard she'd referred to. "Right now they need something to cheer them up."

"I don't think it's a good idea."

"Why not?"

"There are too many of them."

Understanding dawned on Augustus. She was one of the few women among dozens of men. And here he was asking her to flaunt herself for them. Was it any different, really, though, than going to a ball with a dance card dangling from her wrist?

"The men won't touch you." His voice was gruff, even to his own ears. "They know they wouldn't live to see the dawn."

She shook her head. "I still don't think it's a good idea, but I'll do it on one condition."

He grinned at her. "Name your terms."

"If you want me to cheer them up, you have to let me talk to them."

"I don't understand the importance of that."

She smiled sweetly. "Did you feel better after we talked today? After I read the letter."

He narrowed his eyes. "No."

She waited a beat. Then laughed. "Okay. But Granger and Tom seemed to feel better after I talked to them. Don't you agree?"

Reluctantly, he did agree. "I don't know if they felt better or not, but they seemed to enjoy your company."

"I'm good at listening to people."

"I suppose that could be a good skill to have."

She smiled. "It comes in handy from time to time."

Not sure what to make of her response, he turned to the young soldier who'd been volunteered to help him out. His name was Nathaniel and he also served as the drummer boy for Captain Jones' regiment. "Who's next?"

As Augustus removed a bullet from the shoulder of a soldier, he pondered Arabella's request to talk to the men.

He couldn't quite reconcile that she didn't seem to feel safe merely sitting and giving the men someone pleasant to look at, but instead, wanted to spend time talking with them. To Augustus, that seemed like a more dangerous endeavor.

As he dropped the bullet into a tin pan, he glanced in her direction. Already three men had gathered around her and were regaling her with their experiences in today's skirmish. Each one of them seemed eager to tell his story.

Augustus wiped his hands on an already bloodied cloth. Perhaps she wove some magic through her words. Whatever it was she did, he would have to worry about it later. Right now he only had time to hope that none of the wounds he was tending would lead to an amputation.

Augustus reluctantly admitted to himself that he'd been a bit jealous at first. The men flocked to Arabella like bees to honey. She was pretty with her long dark hair and her sultry eyes. But there was something in her expression. Something that the men responded to. Hell, he'd cried in front of her and she'd barely said anything.

She was different from other women. She didn't chatter inanely about things like his sisters' friends. Maybe if he'd socialized more, he would have encountered someone like her.

Even as he had the thought, he dismissed it. There was no one else like Arabella. She was unique.

And just like his fellow soldiers, Augustus was hooked.

CHAPTER 41

$\mathcal{A}$rabella sat perched on a stool next to a soldier and listened as he talked about his dog back home. Her heart went out to him. He was just a boy. A boy who missed his dog.

And now he was on his back, healing from having his head split open from cannon fire.

He'd told her the same story three times now. She suspected that he had some significant brain damage. She could only hope that with proper rest he would recoup enough to live a normal life.

She squeezed his hand and told him she would be back. As someone who spent her life with a bottle of water in her hands, she had to make frequent trips to the well. On top of that, the heat was scorching.

Granger had been assigned the task of minding the well bucket. He was resting his ankle, but had plenty of strength in his arms to move the water bucket up and down inside the well.

Arabella took a long drink and handed the ladle back to

him. She could only hope there was noting seriously contagious going around.

She turned around and nearly bumped right in to Augustus. "I wondered where you'd gotten off to."

She hadn't seen him since yesterday when he'd asked her to *sit and look pretty*. In fact, the more she'd thought about that, the more miffed she'd become.

"Just keeping the soldiers happy like you requested." She started to pass by, but he blocked her path.

"And I'm hearing that you're doing an excellent job."

"That's good to know." She moved the other way, but he blocked her again.

Trying to ignore her racing pulse, she crossed her arms and looked into his deep blue eyes. That was the first mistake. The next was noticing that he hadn't shaved today and he had rolled up the sleeves of his white shirt.

She forgot that she was mad at him and found herself smiling back.

"It's good to see you."

She glanced behind him. "You've been in the tent."

He scowled. "Unfortunately."

She tried to focus. "It must be hot in there."

"We're going to have to move everyone inside."

"Why is that?" The thought of all those soldiers inside the house was daunting to say the least.

"It's going to rain."

Arabella glanced toward the clear blue sky and squinted against the blazing sunlight. "Wishful thinking."

He shook his head. "I don't think so."

She shrugged. "All right." If he wanted to move all these men inside, then he would do it. She was quickly learning that if Augustus Townsend wanted something to happen, it happened.

"I wonder if there's room." She said out loud.

"I'll keep them downstairs."

She thought about her soft bed and how much she was looking forward to sleeping in it tonight. "That's thoughtful." She stood, her feet planted in place. It was pointless to try to move past him.

"There's something else."

"Okay."

"I changed my mind."

"About what?"

"About you looking pretty."

Arabella's stomach dropped. She ran one hand along her soiled skirt. She'd spent some time kneeling in the dirt next to the soldiers. And lowered the brim of her hat with her other hand. "I must look a sight."

He laughed. "No. Not that. You're beautiful. I mean. I want you to help me."

She squinted at him. "What do you need help with?" Surely he didn't think she could help move these men. She could barely navigate the skirts to move herself about. She vowed right then and there that if he was going to ask her to help move the men inside the house, she was going to change back into jeans.

"Help me tend the men. I need a nurse."

"Ha. You just want me to faint again."

He seemed to consider and she felt her face flush with the memory of being in his arms. And she realized she'd been the one to bring it up.

"Not really. I'll be cautious about what I ask you to do. But you seem to do a better of distracting the men than Nathaniel while I stitch and such."

Stitch and such. Dig bullets out of flesh. Amputate fingers. And all manner of unsavory procedures that she'd been hearing about all day. "Okay."

CHAPTER 42

*A*ugustus woke to the sound of birds chirping and the scent of bacon cooking. That meant his father would be heading out to the cotton fields soon and his sisters would be beginning the day's lessons. Even now Adeline was practicing her piano. He knew it was his younger sister Adeline because when Allison played, it sounded like a two-year-old. But Adeline could play. And she was playing even better today than he'd ever heard her play.

He tried to remember what it was he had to do today. Were there any sick neighbors he needed to check in on? He had something he had to do, but he couldn't quite wrap his mind around what it was.

He opened his eyes and struggled to orient himself.

This was not his bedroom.

And it was dusk, not early morning.

He had something to do, alright.

He'd fallen asleep wearing his clothes, covered with blood and with his boots on.

He was in the middle of a war. This stranger's house had essentially become a hospital. The bottom of the house was overflowing with men lying in various states of illness or injury. So far, they'd managed to keep the hospital out of the second story of the house. It was mostly out of respect for the Becquerels who were not even home, but also for selfish reasons. He and Arabella needed a place to escape to. A place that didn't smell like sickness and death.

Arabella. She worked tirelessly alongside him. Her ability to triage was unparalleled. She had some odd ideas about things, especially medicine, but they were saving more men than he'd expected.

Augustus swung his legs over the side of the bed and sat up.

The piano music he'd imagined was still playing. He strained his ears. He wasn't imagining it. Someone was playing the piano and it wasn't his sister. He didn't recognize the song. Unlike the soulful music Adeline always chose, this music was uplifting.

He got up, splashed water on his face, changed into clean clothes, and followed the music downstairs. At the doorway to the parlor, he stopped, and leaned against the doorjamb. Half a dozen men, bandaged and bleeding, stood around the piano and several others, sitting on the floor, were staring toward the piano with rapt attention.

He shifted to see who was playing.

Arabella sat at the piano, her fingers moving deftly along the black and white keys.

Augustus's heart tugged and he fell a little bit more for the strange beauty named Arabella.

CHAPTER 43

Arabella closed her eyes and, sweeping her fingers along the piano keys, allowed herself to be somewhere else. She was at home, in the parlor, taking a break from studying. It was evening, but her grandparents claimed to find her playing both entertaining and soothing. Her grandfather swore up and down that he'd rather spend an evening listening to her playing the piano than watching anything on television. They shared a fierce love of Frank Sinatra.

She lost herself in the sensation of being in a place long ago... yet so very far in the future, allowing the pain of loss to sweep through her, scraping against the edges of her raw emotions.

She finished up Frank Sinatra's *Young at Heart* and moved seamlessly to *New York, New York*, pushing the pain away, pulling herself back to the less distressing present. Makeshift cots filled the bottom floor of the house. The music diminished the moans of men lying in various states of injury. A handful of men, disheveled in their war damaged states, stood around the piano perhaps seeking the music to lift their spirits and perhaps speed their recovery.

The music spilling from beneath her fingertips distracted Arabella from the pain and stench of injury all around her. Some antiseptic was badly needed. Unfortunately, it was about four years away from invention and even further away from widespread use.

After the sound of shuffling and male mumblings registered in her brain, she opened her eyes. Her mind froze, but her fingers kept moving automatically over the black and white keys.

Augustus stood in front of her, watching her from across the piano. She wasn't sure if the other men had stepped away or if his presence merely overshadowed them. It didn't matter.

She saw only him. Her fingers shifted as though of their own accord and without a hitch, she began playing the plaintive strains of *Stardust*, another of her Sinatra favorites.

Their gazes locked and the corners of his lips curved up at the edges in a small smile.

Her breath hitched, but she played the song through. With the last note, the music still lingering in the air, Arabella sat back, her hands in her lap.

Augustus came around the piano, his eyes never leaving hers until he stood about a foot away.

He held out his hand and putting her hand in his, she stood.

With her hand firmly in his grasp, he pulled her out the front door into the darkness of night. Arabella was reminded again. No streetlights. Only the moon to brighten their darkness.

"Did you know it's a blue moon tonight?" He asked.

"A blue moon." She leaned over the railing, but the moon was hidden by the clouds.

"It means it's the second full moon this month."

"I don't even know what day it is, much less what the moon is doing."

He laughed and pulled her with him to sit on the porch swing. "Tell me something."

She turned her head and saw that his face was only inches from hers. "What do want to know?"

"Where are you from?"

A spark of panic shot through her. This was what she'd feared. What she hadn't decided how to answer. The truth was always a good place to start. "Baton Rouge."

"You said you're unmarried?"

"Yes." She thought about her fiancé. And tamped down the surge of guilt about not even having thought about him in days.

"How is that possible?"

"What do you mean?"

He shook his head. "You seem to attract a large number of admirers."

She scoffed. So he seemed to think. "Probably because I'm the only female around."

He laughed. "I don't think that's it."

It wasn't like this at *home.* In her time. In her time, she barely had time to acknowledge men. In fact, most of the men she was in contact with were automatically disqualified as potential love interests. As her favorite professor always said, *clients are not a dating pool.* Nor were colleagues.

Whatever it was, she had no interest in spending time with any of them… except maybe the one she was sitting next to.

As the thought took shape in her mind, he shifted his head and pressed his lips lightly against hers. Held them there.

The world melted away and the only thing she was aware of was the tingles of pleasure that pulsed through her.

He pulled back enough to look into her eyes.

This can't be happening.

This is the past.

CHAPTER 44

$\mathcal{A}$rabella was an angel in the moonlight. His great-grandmother had an old saying. *True love only comes along once in a blue moon.* He'd never taken her literally. He knew that she meant true love only comes rarely. But in this instant, the literal meaning was enmeshed with the metaphorical.

Her lips were so soft just as he'd expected. And she hadn't resisted him. He took that as a positive sign. She was an addiction. An intoxicating drink he couldn't get enough of. He'd thought that true love had passed him by.

But in this inane war, he'd found love.

"I don't think we should do this," she said.

Every bubble of hope he held crashed at his feet. He looked away, staring unseeing into the night.

Such was the way of it. The woman he loved didn't return his favor. "I must apologize."

"Please don't. Please… I"

He turned his gaze back to her. "I understand."

"No. It's just. I live so far away. I don't know how it would work."

"Yet you're here now."

"Yes." Her statement came on a breath and she swayed toward him. He wrapped his arms around her and then their lips were locked.

He just held her, enjoying the sensation, not pressing for more. Arabella was a woman to be savored like a fine wine.

He smiled at himself, his lips moving against hers.

She pulled back. "What? You're smiling."

"I'm happy."

She returned his smile. "I'm happy too."

Then their lips were on each other's again and time stood still.

CHAPTER 45

*A*rabella was lost in the moment. She may be from far, far in the future, but this man was here. Right now. And she wanted to get lost in his arms. Lost in his kiss. Lost in him.

She'd never felt this kind of intensity before. This all consuming passion. This desire to never stop kissing him.

She felt his lips curve into a smile against hers. And, yes, she was happy. Happy to be kissing him. Happy to be here with him in this moment.

It didn't matter how she got here or where she was *supposed* to be. All she knew was that she was where she wanted to be in this moment.

A happy place.

He put an arm beneath her knees and pulled her legs across his lap. In the process, he leaned her back, his arm a cushion for her neck. With the slow moment of the swing, and his lips against hers she felt like she was floating.

This, she thought. *This is what love feels like. This is what brings people to their knees.* Arabella had managed to keep herself emotionally distant from people in spite of her ability to empathize with others. She could offer the practical side to helping people move on from the abyss created in their lives from the absence of love. From this.

Would she be able to do that now, she wondered idly. Or would her level of emotions be forever warped by this experience.

And did it matter? There was no way to know if she would return to her time. There was no way to know if her skills would be needed again. Was it ethical for her to practice psychology in the state of Mississippi? She almost laughed out loud. There was no field of psychology in this time. She was free to do whatever she wanted.

Her feeling of floating intensified and Augustus moved his kisses to the corner of her lips, setting every nerve on fire, then across her cheek to lick lightly at her earlobe.

It occurred to Arabella in that moment, that perhaps she had died and was in heaven.

CHAPTER 46

The hours turned into days and the days into weeks. Vicksburg was under heavy siege and there was nothing they could do to help. The rains continued keeping injured soldiers cooped inside the house. Those that got better moved outside to tents, but without adequate care they seemed to either die or return to the make-shift hospital. Then there were the others. The injured soldiers who found their way to them.

Augustus had thrown many blue jackets into the flames to keep others from knowing which side they fought on. Even so, he wasn't so sure it mattered. The soldiers there in the house under his care were merely trying to survive. They didn't have the strength to fight anyone or anything other than death itself.

Arabella had become his constant companion. She'd held soldiers' hands while he stitched up wounds... while he amputated limbs. And not once had she fainted.

They had fallen into a routine. They worked tirelessly during the day, then ate in the kitchen in the evenings. After supper, sometimes she would play the piano, but often they sat on the porch swing and watched the darkness envelope the land. Those were the best times. Those were the times he could steal kisses. No matter how many he stole, he wanted more.

And they talked. They talked about everything and nothing.

Tonight was no different. Tonight they talked about the war.

Arabella lay with her head in his lap. He toyed with her incredibly soft hair as he listened to her soothing voice.

"How do you know it's not all in vain?"

"The war?" He dragged his fingers out of her hair and caressed her cheeks. "You mean the war has no value?"

He felt her expression brighten beneath his fingertips. He'd picked up some of her vernacular. She told him she'd studied abroad, but when pushed, she wouldn't give him any additional information. It explained in his mind her odd language and at times odd thoughts.

"Exactly. How do you know it has no value?"

"I don't know if war ever has value. It's something men do. Something they have to do. Without war, men would all be fops like the English."

She laughed. "You're saying it keeps their testosterone down."

"Their testo…"

"You know, their need to be aggressive. You're a doctor."

He cleared his throat. A lady wasn't supposed to know of such things, certainly not an unmarried lady. He knew of the testes and their role in sexuality, but he'd never heard of anything called testowhateveritwas. Another of her odd words. He supposed she made them up based off of what she knew which was a great deal. "Yes. I do believe that it gives men something to live for."

"The irony."

"Yes. The downside is that people die. If only there were a way for men to battle without actually having to die."

She tipped her head back and gazed at him. "You're a man ahead of your time."

She'd told him that twice now. The first time was when he insisted on washing his blade between patients.

"Anyway." She entwined her fingers with his free hand. "I hope that your efforts are remembered."

"Why is that?"

"Hundreds of Americans are dying. Don't you want our country's history to be remembered?"

"I don't care if no one remembers me in two hundred years. I don't even care if they remember this inane war. In fact, I hope they don't. There are some things best forgotten. I just try to do the best I can during the life I have to live. I want to make someone's life better. If I can make just one person's life better, I've made my life meaningful."

"You're an unusual man Doctor Colonel Augustus Townsend."

He wasn't sure what she meant by that, but he loved hearing his name on her lips. And he especially loved it when she called him Doctor Colonel or Colonel Doctor which she did frequently, interchanging the order at random.

CHAPTER 47

While Arabella changed her dress for dinner, she wondered as she always did when choosing one from many gowns, about her mother. Did these dresses truly belong to her mother? And if so, how had Arabella ended up in the twentieth century?

Not only was time travel itself illogical, but this situation was inexplicable.

Pulling on a blue dress she hadn't worn before after peeling off one covered in blood and grime, she was thankful for the freed servants who had stayed around to help out. Without them all pulling together to keep the household together, caring for the soldiers would have been impossible.

Though she knew others that did, Arabella never thought of them as slaves. The whole slavery thing was too preposterous to even entertain. Besides, the war wasn't about slavery. It was about states rights. All the soldiers she talked to knew that. She hadn't heard a single man say anything about owning slaves. Even Augustus said that his family hired workers of all races to help them out on their plantation. History got so many things twisted up.

Maybe Augustus was right. Maybe America did need to move on and forget about this time in its history. It was like treating someone with PTSD, she mused. Sometimes it was best to put the incident out of mind and move on. Yes, Augustus was onto something. When… if… when she got back to her time, she would write a paper on that. She'd write that the Civil War needed to be put aside and America needed to move ahead.

Pleased with her thoughts, she studied her reflection in the full-length mirror. She noticed a smile on her face.

And realized that she was happy. She was truly happy.

She had no cell phone. No computer. No electricity. No car. None of the things that were deemed important in the twenty-first century.

Who would have thought that she'd have to travel over one hundred fifty years to find happiness?

CHAPTER 48

Augustus stood on the veranda and watched his men. He smoked a pipe someone had given him along with a rare pouch of tobacco.

He'd made a decision.

A decision that made him ecstatic and terrified all at once.

He wanted to take Arabella home with him. He wanted to show her where he had grown up and where he lived with his family. He wanted her to meet his family. For her to get to know them and them to get to know her. He wanted her to be part of his life. Forever.

In fact, it had gotten to the point that he could no longer imagine his life without her. He could barely remember not knowing her and even now in the midst of this horrid war, he could squint just a little and imagine that instead of soldiers moving about the back lawn, that it was their children who played and laughed. With her, he found himself imagining all sorts of things that had nothing to do with this war.

August had decided to ask for Arabella's hand in marriage.

CHAPTER 49

It was going to rain again. The torrential rains these past few days left them all cooped up inside. Fortunately, the rain brought cooler temperatures with it. Even a breeze now and then. There were dark clouds forming to the west. There was a storm brewing.

Arabella had stepped outside for some fresh air. They'd just lost another one – a man whose amputated leg had become infected. It was a terrible way to go. He'd spent the last days of his life mourning the loss of his limb. This was a most horrible war.

She stood on the veranda and stared unseeing down the dirt road. It had been paved when she drove up. If that wasn't a clue that she was in a different time, nothing was.

She was tired, surviving on mere hours of sleep at a time. There were so many to care for and so few to do the caring. She and Augustus carried the load. He treated the wounds and she treated their hearts.

It was funny how foreign psychology was. She'd known it was a new science – in her time – but seeing the world before was so very odd. Though he didn't get the concept, Augustus seemed to appreciate what she was doing for the men. Just this morning, she'd held a man's hand while Augustus performed an amputation. She still couldn't watch him cutting on anyone with his evil looking saw, but she was getting used to the sounds – unenviable progress.

She noticed a movement in the distance. Even now there was someone coming down the road. It was another wounded soldier making his way toward them. Somehow word had gotten out and there was always another soldier to care for.

With Vicksburg under siege, they were the next safe haven for those outside the walls.

Arabella knew that some of the men they treated were Yankees. Augustus knew it, too, but neither of them talked about it. She wasn't sure anyone even cared anymore. Everyone was tired. Tired from the sickness and death that surrounded them. They all just wanted it to end.

She leaned against the nearest white column and watched the soldier approaching. He wasn't an ordinary soldier. He was an officer. She recognized the uniform and the way he carried himself. Yet he was alone and he was walking, albeit with a limp.

When he reached the bottom of the stairs, he stopped and gazed up at her.

He didn't speak. Instead he peered at her with that same intensity that she'd first encountered with Villars. It was as though he recognized her.

The wind swept her hair across her cheeks and she pulled it back and held it with one hand.

The raindrops began falling as the man stood staring at her.

"Come." She motioned with her hand for him to come up to the veranda. "You'll be soaked."

He didn't move and for a moment she thought he might be suffering from a PTSD flashback or as they called it here, shellshock.

His eyes still locked onto hers, he took one step up. It was raining now.

She couldn't allow this man to stand there when he could be underneath the shelter of the veranda. He was obviously not well to begin with. Standing in the rain would only make it worse.

She pulled her skirts up over her ankles and walked down the steps, took his arm, and tugged gently. He stayed frozen in place. She looked up, her hair and clothes getting soaked by the moment and met his gaze. He was older than she – perhaps in his mid-fifties. His face wore the shadow of a beard, but it was his eyes that caught her attention.

His eyes looked familiar.

She shook off the sensation. Her great-grandmother's influence was ever present.

There was no way that she could know someone living in this time. The thought was so ridiculous that she laughed out loud.

Then the man swayed and began to fall. She tried, but she couldn't stop him. He was too heavy. He'd fainted. And he pulled her down with him.

CHAPTER 50

*A*ugustus heard a commotion out back. It wasn't the usual commotion – the one men make just being men. Besides he knew Arabella had gone outside to get some air.

He dropped the needle he'd been threading and dashed toward the back, his long legs eating up the space, his heart pumping furiously.

When he saw her on the ground, pushing at the soldier pinning her down, his first thought was the he was about to have to kill someone.

But as he flew down the stairs, he realized that the man had passed out and Arabella was merely trying to disengage herself.

The soldier was big, at least as big as he was, but he managed to roll him over and then helped Arabella pull her skirt free.

"What happened?"

"He fainted. I don't think he's well."

"Go find someone to help me get him inside." The rain was coming down in torrents now and Augustus could barely see with the rain splashing in his eyes.

Arabella dashed up the stairs and disappeared inside.

Augustus tried to give the man a cursory examination, but all he could really tell was that he had a pulse.

A minute later, two soldiers grabbed him up and hauled him inside the house. All of them walked through dripping water onto the hardwood floors. They put him in the study and Arabella reluctantly went upstairs to change out of her dress. She could barely move around in all those skirts soaked as she was.

Augustus determined that the man had an infection in his leg. He sat back and sighed. That would mean another amputation.

The man blinked and opened his eyes. "Home." The word came on parched lips.

"Yes," Augustus agreed. "You're inside."

The man shook his head. "Home." He insisted before his eyes closed again.

CHAPTER 51

*A*rabella had been through so many dresses she'd lost count. It was a good thing the lady of the house had lots of clothes. And it was good thing they were the same size.

It would all make sense if she were truly Ericka, Arabella's mother. But no matter how much she tried to make sense of that, she couldn't wrap her head around it.

It makes as much sense as you being here in 1863.

Every time her thoughts bumped up against the whole notion, she hit a wall. It just wasn't plausible. It was too much to accept that she had travelled through time, much less that her mother was here in this century still living.

She toweled off her hair and combed it through. She hated for Augustus to see her looking like a soaked rat. But there was no time for it to dry. Not with a new patient downstairs. One who obviously was going to need some type of treatment.

After putting on a green dress with a black sash, she put on her pair of boots, and headed back downstairs. A group of soldiers were playing cards and telling jokes. At least their morale was good. She'd never thought about the extent of boredom for the wounded and healthy alike during the days they were waiting for their next order.

She stepped into the study and found Augustus scowling at the man's leg. She inhaled sharply. Even she could see the beginning signs of infection spreading from his injury.

"It's bad." She tugged the man's knapsack off his back to allow him to lie back more comfortably. "I wonder how far he walked."

"There's no telling. Men will walk all across the country just to make their way home."

"It's like an instinct." She mused, kneeling next to the man and wiping dirt from his face. The thought came back unbidden. He looked familiar. "How long can you wait before you have to amputate?" She asked him that every time. She'd asked him to try other treatment methods, but he insisted it was the only way to keep them alive. Many died anyway.

Augustus sat on the desk, studying the man from across the room. He shook his head and swiped his wet hair off his face. "I don't know." His voice sounded defeated. Resigned. "Three days at the longest."

She always asked him what the longest time was. "But you want to do it now."

"I don't want to do it. But I know it's inevitable."

"There's got to be another way." The words were automatic and she no longer even expected him to respond.

"I wish to God above there was."

She looked at him sharply. "There is."

"My eternal optimist."

Every time she came close to telling him where… when she was from, he gave her an excuse not to. He'd picked up a book from the desk and flipped through the pages.

Arabella turned back and continued to study the man's features.

The man blinked and opened his eyes. He held her gaze. His lips curved in a smile. Perhaps he was dreaming.

"Arabella," he whispered.

CHAPTER 52

ugustus heard Arabella fall back onto her backside and was off the desk in an instant. What had happened now?

The man's eyes were open.

Arabella tried to stand, but kept stepping on her skirts, pulling her back to the floor.

"Here." He took her arms. "Here. Let me help you. What happened?"

He helped her stand, but she didn't take her eyes off the man. Her eyes were wide and she watched him warily as she would a rabid dog.

"Did he hurt you?"

That seemed to jar her out of the trance. "No. No, of course not."

"What then? You look like you've seen a ghost."

"I have."

"Arabella." The man said more loudly.

Augustus looked at her. "You know this man?"

"No." She shook her head.

"He knows you."

Her fingertips were digging into his arm as she held onto him. "I have to…" She stopped. Glanced at him, then back at the man on the floor. "I have to do something."

With that, she gathered up her skirts and ran from the room.

Augustus watched her leave, then turned to his patient.

"Whiskey."

Augustus scoffed. "What I would give for a swig right now."

The man scanned the room and attempted to sit up.

"Whoa. We'll get you dried off and something to eat before you try to get up." He picked up a towel and handed it to the man.

He wiped his face and ran the towel over his hair. "There." He pointed. "On the third shelf from the top. There's a bottle of whiskey."

Augustus suspected the man had been become addled from the infection.

"Just look." He insisted.

Augustus went to where the man pointed, moved some books aside, and there he found a bottle of whiskey. He slid it off the shelf and turned questioningly back to the wounded soldier.

"Charles Becquerel," he said. "This is my house."

CHAPTER 53

*A*rabella ran upstairs, nearly losing her footing. She could barely see through the tears that glazed her eyes. *No. It can't be.* She repeated the phrase over and over as she ran.

She reached her room, threw open the trunk and pulled out the picture of the little family. She missed inside lighting probably more than anything else. With the clouds, there was no light coming from outside either.

She took the picture with her to the bedside and held it near the candlelight.

"I need a magnifying glass."

She looked around for something that might magnify. *My phone!*

She dashed to the bureau where she'd hidden her phone and switched it on. It still had twenty percent.

Propping the picture beneath the candle, she took a picture as close she could get it. Then she went into her phone, zoomed in, and could see their features much more clearly.

"Her eyes are like mine. And our lips are the same." They even had the same little freckle on their left cheek.

She scanned over to the image of the man. "And I have his nose." That's why he looked familiar.

She sat back on the bed, staring at the picture on her phone. The man had seen the resemblance to the woman. Except for their noses, they were mirror images.

It was true then.

Her parents lived.

CHAPTER 54

Augustus found Arabella in her room, sitting in the middle of her bed, staring at… something. Perhaps the photograph he'd seen her looking at more often than he knew.

She was staring so intently she didn't hear him come in.

He peered over her shoulder. She was looking at the images, but they were bigger and on some kind of glass. He watched as she put her fingers on the glass and the images got even bigger.

He must have made a sound because she gasped and hid it behind her.

"What is that?"

"Nothing." Her answer came quickly telling him it was something.

"Let me see."

"No. I can't."

Witchcraft had been discredited. Hadn't it? "Are you a witch then?"

She scoffed. "You know better."

"How?"

"If I were a witch, your patients wouldn't die."

"Good point." He waited, watching her expectantly, but she didn't budge. "So can I see?"

She brought the glass out and held it up for him. He'd been right. It was the same picture. "How?"

"It's a camera. I took a picture of the picture."

"I don't understand."

She hesitated, then said. "Here. Let me show you." She leaned toward him, pressing her cheek against his, held the glass in front of them to show their reflections and touched it.

Then she showed him the glass. There was an image of the two of them on it. He reached out as though to touch it, but pulled his hand back.

"It's okay. You can hold it." Holding it by its sides, she handed him the glass.

He took it from her, careful not to touch the reflective glass. "Will it disappear if you touch the image?"

She nodded. "Yes."

"How long will it stay this way?"

"Not much longer, I'm afraid."

"But you touched it before."

She sighed. "Yes. But very lightly." She put two fingers on it and suddenly his image was the only one there and it was much bigger.

He stared at his reflection. "I need to shave."

She laughed.

Then suddenly the picture dimmed. And a second later, it faded completely, leaving only a black mirror. She took it from his hands. "It's out of energy."

"What gives it energy?"

Thunder rumbled in the distance as she seemed to consider. "It's like kerosene for a lantern. Only it's able to hold onto energy for a few minutes without the flame. Then it goes out."

He frowned. "How does it get more energy?"

She glanced at the window. "Sunlight. So it won't work now." She put it in her skirt pocket.

"Oh, I came up here to tell you something about our newest patient."

She looked into his eyes. "His name is Charles Becquerel and I think he's my father."

CHAPTER 55

Arabella wiped her hands on her skirt as she walked down the hallway with Augustus. Her hoop skirt swayed slightly. She was getting the hang of maneuvering the hoops. When they reached the top of the landing, the grandfather clock began tolling the hour.

She was nervous. It was very likely that she was about to meet her father. The father she had believed to be dead her whole life.

It was strange though that he didn't seem particularly surprised to see her. She would have to ponder that further, but right now her heart was beating too fast for her to think straight. As they reached the landing, a flash of lightening shot through the window in front of them. Arabella grabbed Augustus' hand and jumped back.

"It's all right. The ..." He assured her. But the rumble of thunder drowned out the rest of his words.

They continued down the stairs as the storm crashed around them. When they reached the bottom of the stairs, the grandfather clock chimed the eighth time, but its echo lingered as they passed in front of it.

"I'll be right back," Augustus said, releasing her hand, and turning away.

"Wait." Arabella called. She suddenly felt dizzy with an aura that she was about to faint again. "Augustus."

He turned back to catch her. She saw his outstretched hands, but then there was nothing.

CHAPTER 56

Arabella woke to sound of a power saw.

A power saw.

She lay very still, not moving. The power saw stopped, but then she heard… sounds. Normal sounds. The roar of an air conditioner. The hum of a refrigerator. Music. Someone was jamming out to Brett Young's *In Case you Didn't Know*.

A range of emotions tumbled over each other. Relief. She was home. Excitement. She was back to her own time.

She opened her eyes. She was back on the couch. The grandfather clock was silent. She clutched the key around her neck.

Heartbreak.

She was no longer in 1863.

CHAPTER 57

Augustus grabbed for Arabella as he watched her fall to the floor. But instead of catching her, he caught an armful of air.

He stumbled. Caught himself, then turned in a circle three times.

She wasn't there.

She'd vanished in front of him.

No!

He dropped to his knees. Arabella. His love. His life.

Where did she go?

"She'll come back."

Augustus jerked his head up. Charles was leaning against the doorjamb. "You shouldn't be up." The words were automatic. He'd said them a thousand times. He struggled to find the words to ask the next question. "Where did she go?"

"Come with me." Charles said. "I'll see if I can explain it."

Augustus got to his feet and followed his host back to the study. Charles poured a shot of whiskey and handed it to him.

Augustus swallowed, feeling the burn all the way to his gut.

He held out the glass. Charles chuckled and poured. Then put the cork back in the bottle and set it aside.

"Arabella is my daughter." He said and Augustus heard the pride in his voice.

"I know."

"Oh. Does she know?"

"I think so. Yes."

Charles nodded. And sat in the big leather chair behind the desk. His face contorted in pain.

"You shouldn't be up."

"I know. I want to get all the use out my leg before you take it off."

Augustus held up his glass. Then drank the whiskey. "Good point. Tell me where your daughter went. Please." Augustus sat in the chair opposite Charles. He felt like someone had punched him in the gut and he couldn't quite catch his breath.

"She's from the future."

Augustus inhaled deeply. "I think I misunderstood."

Charles shook his head. "Technically she was born here… in this time, but through an accident, she went forward in time."

Augustus scoffed. "How can someone *accidentally* go forward in time?

But he thought about her strange dress when he'd first met her – she'd been wearing men's trousers. He thought about the magic glass that captured their images. The way Villars had reacted to seeing her.

Those were things that couldn't be ignored. And most of all, he couldn't ignore that he'd seen her disappear in front of his eyes.

"I was out in the fields," Charles began. "My wife, Ericka, was here with Arabella." He put his fingers over his eyes. Then continued. "Arabella was four months old. Ericka's brother Bradley and Camille had just married. So the two women were here as well as Ericka's great-grandmother, Vaughn. Ericka went upstairs to take a bath, leaving Arabella with Camille and Vaughn.

"Bradley came home early and Camille rushed out to see him. Before she left, she handed Arabella off to Vaughn." Charles lifted his head and Augustus could see the pain in them. "We never saw either one of them again. We tore this place apart, inside and out, but they were gone."

"Where did they go?" Even as he asked, he knew what Charles was going to say.

"There was only one explanation. Vaughn had traveled through time and had taken Arabella with her."

"For God's sake man."

"It nearly tore us all apart. Ericka was from the future, too, but from what Vaughn said, once someone is with their soul mate, they stay put. So Erika couldn't go get her. It wasn't from lack of trying, mind you."

"I can't imagine the hell this family must have gone through."

Charles nodded. "We survived. I never doubted I would see my daughter again. But it's been so long. She looks so much like Ericka did at that age. I knew her immediately."

"Only to lose her again," Augustus said quietly.

"Yes. Only to lose her again." Charles studied Augustus. "What is your relationship to my daughter?"

Augustus felt his eyes widen under the scrutiny of Arabella's father. "I was planning to marry her."

"Why?"

"What do you mean?"

"Don't be daft. Men marry for a variety of reasons. When I met Ericka I was engaged to another woman. My own father had arranged the marriage for business reasons."

"I don't have any business with her."

"Some men marry because they don't want to be alone or

just because they want a pretty face around. Someone to scratch their itch."

Augustus flushed. He'd talked with men often enough about *itches,* but this was the father of the woman he loved. "It's not like that."

"Do you love her?"

"More than anything."

"How do you know?"

Augustus stood up and filled his glass with whiskey. After drinking the liquor, he squared his shoulders and turned to Charles. "I love everything about her. Her beauty. Her laugh. The way she can make a man feel better just by listening to him talk. I get drunk on her kisses and I can't stand to be apart from her for more than minutes at a time."

Charles shifted, leaned back and propped his leg on a stack of books. He winced. "Does she know this?"

Augustus went to the window, his back to Charles. "I haven't told her." *I should have told her how I feel.* And now it was too late. *I never should have let go of her hand.*

CHAPTER 58

Arabella gathered up her skirts and dashed upstairs, ran down the hallway, and looked into each of the rooms. They were much as she had last seen them – in this time – paint cans, no furniture.

What had Jerry done with her luggage?

She ran back downstairs, her heat beating frantically. Her mind echoing one word over and over. *No!*

She found her suitcase in the parlor, tucked in the corner where she had left it. She put her hand to her forehead. *Think.* She inhaled deeply. Slowly. Her hands trembling, she knelt and unzipped her suitcase. There tucked beneath her tee-shirts was the folded up letter that Vaughn had written.

She took it with her to the couch and sat down as she unfolded it and read it for the thousandth time.

She could only make out a few words from the bottom half of the letter. The part where her tears had permanently smudged the ink.

Clock. Time. You were a baby...

I wish... back.

She groaned in frustration and crumpling the paper, dropped her hands into her lap.

"Miss Arabella?"

Arabella jerked her head around. Jerry stood behind her, watching her warily.

"Jerry." Arabella was suddenly self-conscious of her long dress. She stood up and hid her hands in her skirts.

"Are you okay?" He asked.

No. "Yes."

"What are you doing?"

"Oh. Um." She forced a laugh. "There's a reenactment…"

"Right. It's that time of the year." He scrubbed his chin. "Your boyfriend was looking for you. You might want to give him a call."

Arabella slipped a hand into her pocket and wrapped her fingers around her cell phone. "I didn't have my charger."

"Okay. Well…" He seemed unsure what to do. "I'll be out back running a few boards. If you need anything."

Arabella collapsed on the sofa and pulled out her cell phone. She pressed the power button and watched as it lit up. She had fifty messages and about a million texts.

Instead of playing them, she put the phone on the console table where she'd left her charger, plugged in the phone and went down the hall to take a shower.

CHAPTER 59

"It's time for us to go."

Augustus glanced over at Captain Jones sitting on the veranda. "Surely not to Vicksburg."

"We have to."

"It's a lost cause, you know."

"It may be a lost cause, but it's our lost cause."

Augustus nodded. He understood completely. How many lost causes had he fought for? Men that he knew wouldn't survive. A few of them did and that made it all worthwhile.

"Do you want to come with us?"

Augustus knew that he should. They were no longer needed here. His men were rested and well fed which was more than most of the officers could say about their troops.

But he couldn't leave here. Not without Arabella.

Charles' words rang in his ears. *She'll come back.* It was a phrase he repeated to himself over and over. "I'm still needed here."

Captain Jones nodded. "You've done some good work."

"It's been a lot. But there are still men who need to be treated. And they keep coming."

Captain Jones laughed. "Somehow word got out. It's almost like a little hospital here."

It was, Augustus thought, when Arabella was here. Now it was just a place with a bunch of sick soldiers. He would never say that out loud though. It would sound almost treasonous. Like he didn't want to be here. And without Arabella, being here had no meaning, but then being anywhere without her would be meaningless.

The only hopefulness was that Arabella's father was here. Augustus had told Charles everything he knew about her. Well almost everything. He didn't tell him about the hours they'd spent kissing on this very veranda.

"We'll leave at dawn," Captain Jones said, breaking into Augustus' thoughts.

"I wish you the best,"Augustus said.

He would stay here. Right here in this house and wait for Arabella. He would wait for her as long as it took for her to return to him.

Even if it meant he spent the rest of his life here.

CHAPTER 60

$\mathcal{F}$eeling oddly out of place, Arabella sat on the sofa and played her messages. She took notes as she went. The receptionist from the ER called everyday for about a week, then stopped. There were a couple of telemarketing calls. The bank called to remind her about a credit card payment – the only one that wasn't automated.

The rest of the calls were from Matthew Caldwell Jennings, III. She wasn't sure why she always thought of her fiancé by his full name. Maybe it was because the name fit him so well. He was very formal and always wanted things just so.

She'd found that cute at first. The way he was always well dressed and didn't like to walk on grass because he'd get his shoes dirty.

She had a vivid memory of Augustus hugging her, both of them covered other men's blood. Messy. The work Augustus did was messy.

And somewhere along the way, she'd become desensitized to it. She still turned away when he cut into someone, but she could clean someone up and think nothing of it.

She wondered what he was doing now. Had he seen her vanish?

How had it happened? She remembered calling out to him and reaching for his hand. What was he thinking?

And then there was the man that was likely her father.

She grabbed up her phone and googled Charles Becquerel. Nothing.

What had happened to him?

He died when you were an infant.

Ericka went to stand at the window. The heat from the sun was unbearable. It was nothing like the torrential rains they'd been having in 1863.

I must have been dreaming. But she'd lost three weeks. If she'd been asleep for three weeks, surely Jerry would have called the ambulance to come get her. He'd seemed surprised to see her. But he had taken her dress in stride.

It was too much to think about. And there was no one to talk to about it. *My father. I need to talk to my father.*

Maybe I need to check myself into the psych ward.

With a flash of inspiration, she opened her phone, went to photos and found the picture she'd taken.

The selfie of her and Augustus. The live feature had been on. She pressed the image and saw him take a breath.

Augustus had been real.

And if Augustus had been real, if she could accept that fact, she had to accept that she had really been in 1863.

CHAPTER 61

"Let me see it." Augustus gestured toward Charles' leg.

"You just looked at it this morning."

"Yes, but I want to see it again."

Charles sighed and allowed Augustus to look at his leg – puffy and discolored with infection.

"I'm gonna have to take it."

"Not until Erika gets here."

"That could be weeks."

"Then we'll wait weeks."

"What do you expect her to do?"

"I don't know. But she'll think of something."

Augustus pressed on the wound. "Because she's from the future. That doesn't make her a doctor."

"No. But she knows a lot of things."

"We'll wait a little longer, but I won't have you dying on me."

"Being without a leg may be worse," Charles murmured.

"Many men before you have said the same thing. And many men have adapted to life without a limb."

"I don't think I could. Besides, don't most people die

anyway?" He continued when Augustus stared at him blankly. "So you're going to haggle me up to keep from dying and I'm going to die anyway."

"Your daughter said almost the same words."

Charles smiled as he always did when they talked about Arabella.

The mere mention of her name nearly sent Augustus spiraling. He could barely eat for missing her. He couldn't eat and he couldn't sleep.

He thought about her all the time. He vowed to himself that if she ever came back, he would declare his love immediately. If it were up to him, he'd take her from this house. But he knew that neither she nor her parents would allow that to happen. No, he mused, *either way, I'm destined to live out my days here.* Either waiting for her to return or living life with her here.

"I understand the hell you're going through." Charles pulled the sheet back over his leg. "I went through the same thing with Ericka. I thought I'd lost her forever."

"How did you cope?" Cope. Arabella had even changed his vocabulary. She often spoke of helping the men with their coping skills.

Charles scoffed. "Horrendously. No one could tolerate being around me. I spent my time brooding and staying alone in my garconniere. I came around occasionally to read to my little sister, but it wasn't long before she sent me away for making her fairy tales sound like horror stories. The worst part was that I was actually going to marry someone else – Anna."

"I can't even imagine wanting to be with anyone besides Arabella."

"I no longer cared. I knew then that she'd gone back to the future and I was convinced that I would never see her again in this lifetime"

"But she came back?"

"Yes. It was quite dramatic. Like something out of a

fairytale. I was at the altar next to Anna when I saw Ericka standing in the back of the church.

"Good God."

"It was a miracle." Charles' eyes filled with unshed tears and he looked away. It was our love that brought us back together."

Augustus had seen this before. Sometimes the infection was so bad that it began to affect the mind.

Perhaps he'd waited too long to do the amputation.

CHAPTER 62

*A*rabella roamed aimlessly around the big plantation house. She was having a hard time wrapping her head around all that had happened. She wished fervently for her great-grandmother. Vaughn could explain everything and make sense of it all. If only she had talked to Arabella about this before her death.

She brushed off Jerry's attempts to engage her in conversation. Since Vaughn wasn't there, she just wanted to be left alone.

She plundered through the room with all the furniture shoved against each other. It was highly inconvenient. Especially since she was pretty sure the wardrobe in the corner was the same one she'd used in 1863.

"Jerry," she called. "I need to get in this bureau. Will you help me?"

Jerry blew out a breath, but went to work moving aside four other heavy pieces of furniture. "What are you looking for?"

"I don't know."

As soon as he had the doors free, she threw them open, more than halfway expecting to see her jeans and tee-shirt stacked on the third shelf where she'd left them. Instead it was empty.

"Are you looking for something that belonged to your great-grandmother?"

"Yes." Anything that would give her some glimpse into the past she'd left behind.

"Most everything got stored in the attic. There's a bunch of old trunks up there."

"There are trunks in the attic?" Of course. It made perfect sense. So many people had lived here over the years, things would naturally have been packed away and stored.

"Yeah."

"Where's the attic?"

After Jerry led her to the attic door, she stood in awe at so many things she'd used when she was in the past. There was the full-length mirror and a vanity that had been in her room. And there, shoved against the wall was the trunk.

She threw open the lid and rummaged through. She found the same tintype she'd seen before. The one with her parents holding her as an infant. But nothing seemed to have been added.

Disappointed, she closed the trunk, stood up, and looked around. There was a smaller trunk that didn't look familiar. It looked newer – more modern.

She opened the lid and found a stack of books. One was a journal written by Christopher Becquerel. She'd read that later.

Another brought a catch to her breath. The family Bible. It took both hands to drag the heavy book out of the trunk. She went quickly to the list of births and deaths. Most of the names she didn't recognize.

But two of them, she did.

Ericka Becquerel. *Died 1901.*

Charles Becquerel. *Died June 12, 1863 from infection resulting from leg amputation.*

"No!" Her hands trembling, she sat back and stared straight ahead, past the spider webs and sunlight streaming in through the little dormer windows.

She had been there. She had met her father.

Not only had she met her father in 1863, but she had fallen in love. She had fallen in love with the man who killed her father.

CHAPTER 63

Augustus made his last entry for the day and closed his journal. He would have to provide an accounting of all his patients when he was reunited with the main army. He would be reprimanded for not sending a report already, but he wanted his men here. Not only were their numbers dwindling fast, but also the reports coming out of Vicksburg were disturbing to say the least.

A part of him regretted not being there to help out with the siege, but another part of him, a much larger part was relieved that he and his men weren't trapped in the hell that was Vicksburg. He'd heard that the civilians had taken to hiding out in caves in order to survive the shelling. The idea was preposterous.

He poured a glass of sherry and sat in front of the window. There was a breeze tonight, offering a much needed respite from the insufferable heat. It was no wonder men were dying right and left. Marching around in heavy uniforms in this heat.

He swirled his drink and embraced his overall general bad mood. He missed Arabella. He missed her with every breath.

He longed to feel her soft lips against his. To hear her laugh.

To hear her ideas. She was by far the most intelligent woman he had ever met. She'd said she went to college for quite some time. She'd told him that she'd learned to be a good listener in college.

He supposed it was possible. One of those woman things like embroidering and knitting. How did one study listening anyway? He couldn't deny that it was effective. Grown men would tell her anything. Himself included.

Now that he'd talked with Charles, he wanted to learn more about her life in the future.

A knock at the door interrupted his thoughts.

"Sir, Mister Charles requested that you come downstairs."

Augustus set down his drink and slid into his shoes. He'd begun to think of Charles as more of a friend than a patient. That was never a good idea. His objectivity had blurred and he'd allowed Charles' infection to go on longer than he should have. He only prayed it didn't cost him his life. When – not if – Arabella returned, he didn't want it on his head to have to tell her what happened to him.

He padded down the hallway and made his way down the stairs as the grandfather clock chimed nine times. He was normally sitting with Arabella around this time each night. It was astounding how quickly she'd become part of his life.

He reached the study where Charles slept on a pallet on the floor. His friend did not look well. He looked pale and weak. More so than this morning when Augustus had last seen him.

"Doc," Charles said. Charles never called him Doc. It was always Augustus. Something was not right.

"Villars said you asked for me."

"Yes." He shifted and grimaced. "It's time. It's time for you to take my leg."

CHAPTER 64

*A*rabella had things to do. Spurred into action by the knowledge that her father was about to die – in 1863 - inadvertently at the hand of the man she loved, she made some phone calls. She called in a favor from a physician assistant at the ER where she worked. It took doing to navigate the questions about where she'd been, but finally, her friend cooperated.

She made a flying trip to the local pharmacy to pick up a prescription for augmentin, and grabbed some iodine antiseptic off the shelf. Such simple things that could so easily save a life. If only they were available.

The girl behind the counter informed her that it would be another hour before the antibiotic prescription would be ready. Arabella walked around the store twice, then stepped outside and took pictures of her car with her phone. She also took pictures of the downtown street crawling with pedestrians as well as other vehicles.

Unable to think of anything else to pass the time, she went back and sat in a chair near the pharmacy counter.

She was immediately drawn back to the picture she'd taken

of her and Augustus. His look of bewilderment would have been funny if it had been anyone else. Instead, it brought tears to her eyes. She loved his silky dark hair, his face with an almost perpetual five o'clock shadow. She knew he shaved when he could, but didn't take the time to shave daily.

She touched the image of his oh so kissable lips and longed to feel them on hers again. Even in the picture, she could see how perfectly, her head fit beneath his chin. She imagined the way his strong arms wrapped around her and held her close. Safe.

Please my love. Please don't do it. Don't kill my father.

She couldn't hate Augustus for it. It wasn't his fault. It was merely what physicians did in that time. The same people of the future would read about chemo and shake their heads. They'll wonder how people could been so…

"Miss Becquerel."

Arabella jumped up, closed her phone and dashed to the counter. Finally. She needed to get back to the house.

Now came the hard part.

How on earth was she going to get back to 1863?

CHAPTER 65

A group of wounded soldiers came to their doorstep the next day and interrupted Augustus' plan to amputate Charles' leg.

Although Augustus knew he could have the leg off in a matter of ten minutes, he welcomed the delay. Although he knew it might save the man's life, he also knew that it carried risks. Risks and a life of being unwhole.

Once a limb was taken from a man, he was never the same again. Especially a man like Charles. A man who spent time every day on a horse, minding his plantation.

The damnable war had completely destroyed a way of life. Not just for the soldiers, but for each family and even each individual who was touched by it. And could anyone living in the south not be touched by the war? It came to their doorstep and forced its way inside.

He'd taken care of all the men. There was no further reason to delay. Nonetheless, Augustus dragged his feet to the study. When he peeked into the room, he saw that Charles was sleeping peacefully. "Well hell." He backed quietly out of the room. How long had it been since the man had a good sleep?

He wasn't about to wake him from what could be delightful dreams only to saw his damn leg off.

He stopped by the kitchen for a glass of cold lemonade and went to sit on the back porch. The lemons reminded him of his friend Stonewall Jackson. *Let's meet on the other side of the river,* he had said upon his death.

Augustus could only hope that he could meet his own death with such dignity. War. Augustus hated this war. Everything about it.

But mostly he missed Arabella. She had been the one who could liven his mood with just a glance and her smile had brightened his world.

Augustus was no good without her. She'd come into his life and branded his heart. Without her, he floundered. No purpose. No joy. When she left, she took the light with her.

CHAPTER 66

Arabella sat on the couch reading Christopher Becquerel's journal. Christopher had given up his birthright as the oldest son to chase his dream of being a soldier. He'd left Charles in an impossible situation as a result – feeling forced to marry a woman he didn't love.

Nonetheless, there had been a happy ending. Her father had found her mother. Or she had found him. However it worked.

She wondered what Christopher was doing now. Was he fighting in the Civil War? She corrected herself. Had he fought in the war?

It was difficult to remember that the war was not being fought at this very moment when her heart and soul were in 1863.

Here in 2018, she had nothing. No parents. No grandparents. No siblings. No family at all to keep her here. All she had was her work and she was fairly certain that bridge had been burned. Only now did she realize how much her life revolved around her work. She'd been absent without leave. Other than calling on her friend for some antibiotics, she'd made no phone call. No text. Nothing. Certainly no paperwork for time off. She scoffed at the inanity of it all.

A man's very life hung in the balance. And not just any man. Her father.

She set the journal aside and stretched out on the sofa. Perhaps she'd take a nap. She adjusted her skirts, checking her pockets as she'd done a hundred times over the past two days. She finally tacked them together with safety pins so nothing would fall out. In her left pocket, she had the bottle of antibiotics and the antiseptic. In her right pocket she had her cell phone and a little battery pack for charging. She hadn't changed clothes for two days. If she went back in time, she wanted to make certain she had the medicine needed for her father.

She had no explanation for wanting to take the cell phone.

She closed her eyes and allowed her thoughts to wander back to Augustus. She missed him. Missed everything about him.

Someone was at the door. She waited for Jerry to get it. Jerry must have been out back because he didn't seem to hear the person knocking.

They knocked again. Louder this time.

Groaning, she pulled herself off the sofa. She'd just been on the edge of sleep in that wonderful place where everything was good.

She opened the front door.

And stood face-to-face with Matthew Caldwell Jennings, III.

"My God, Arabella!" His face was contorted in anger. "Where the hell have you been?"

Arabella turned and without answering, walked away from him.

He grabbed her arm, stopping her. "What in God's name are you wearing?"

She jerked her elbow from his hand and glanced down at her long dress. It was one of her favorites. It was a dark green with a black sash around the waist. The color reminded her of the dress Scarlett had made out of her mother's portieres in *Gone with the Wind*. The dress had a high neckline which was particularly comfortable and nonrevealing when tending to soldiers. She was wearing a wired caged crinoline, moderate in size, and she'd learned to maneuver it quite well. She liked the way the hoop swayed slightly around her when she walked. She was wearing her own lace up boots and considered herself to be tastefully dressed.

She lifted her chin. "What are you doing here?"

He crossed his arms. "Looking for you." He ran his eyes down to the bottom of her skirt and back up again. "You've been missing for over three weeks. You haven't been at work. You haven't answered my calls. Nothing."

She scowled at him. "I'm over twenty-one."

"Where's your ring?"

CHAPTER 67

"Go ahead and do it already."

Augustus studied his friend Charles lying in the huge poster bed. Yesterday, he had had some soldiers carry Charles up to his bedroom – the bedroom Arabella had been sleeping in.

Though Charles was beneath two heavy blankets, he was still having chills. "You were adamant about waiting for your wife to get here."

"And you were adamant about the urgency of doing the amputation." Charles was feverish and he was weak, the dark blotches under his eyes making him look older.

Augustus didn't have the heart to tell him. Taking his leg wasn't going to save him. They'd waited too long. Augustus had been swayed by personal feelings and now Charles was paying the ultimate price.

His life.

CHAPTER 68

Her ring.

Arabella glanced down at her ringless hand. She'd completely forgotten. The ring he'd given her was too large, so she'd taken it to the jewelry shop to have it resized. It had completely slipped her memory to pick it up. "It's being resized, remember?"

"That was months ago."

"I've been preoccupied."

"Have you joined one of those re-enactor groups? I saw a group dressed like you on my way through downtown."

"And if I have?"

"Why are you embarrassing me like this?"

"What I do has nothing to do with you."

"Have you gone insane? We're engaged to be married. You didn't even bother to be there for the charity event. I'm trying to make partner."

"It's all about you."

"That's right. You said you'd help me."

"Well, that was before," she said softly.

Matthew scoffed. "Before what? Before you lost your mind?"

"There's no need to be offensive." She kept her voice low.

"I never thought you'd run off to join one of those reenacting groups."

"I never took you to be an asshole."

He grabbed her arm again. This time his fingers ground around her wrist. "Stop it. You're hurting me." She tugged away and her sleeve ripped as her arm twisted.

"Hey!" Jerry called from the back door. "What's going on?"

"I'm taking her out of here." He turned and started pulling her with him toward the door.

"No." Arabella's eyes were moist from the pain in her arm.

"Let her go." Jerry stepped forward and grabbed Matthew by the collar, jerking his head back.

"Quit it, old man."

Jerry punched him in the jaw. He released Arabella and she fell to the floor.

As Matthew rubbed his jaw, Jerry stood face-to-face with him. "You busted my lip!"

"Yeah, you hurt her wrist."

Matthew scoffed.

Jerry punched him again, this time in the stomach. "Don't you ever put your hands on a woman again."

"I'm her fiancé."

"All the more reason for you to protect her, not hurt her, you idiot."

Jerry turned to Arabella. "Do you want him around?"

She massaged her wrist while trying to hold her hoop skirt down. She was contemplating how she was going to get off the floor while tangled in her hoop and skirts. She looked up at Matthew – the man she'd agreed to marry.

As she studied the man wearing a paisley tie and navy suit jacket, she didn't really know him. They'd seemed compatible at first, then they'd fallen into a routine. Date night on Friday. Other than that they mostly saw each other only at social events, like the charity event she'd apparently missed. "I think he needs to go."

Jerry turned him around, pointed him toward the door.

"I want my ring back." Matthew said over his shoulder.

"You can pick it up at the jewelry store." She said, but she wasn't sure he even heard her. It didn't matter. Jerry shoved him out the door and came to help her off the floor. "Thank you. You're a good man Jerry."

Jerry escorted her back to the sofa. He hadn't made any comments about the way she was dressed. "It's what we do. We take care of family."

CHAPTER 69

Augustus sat out on the veranda in the swing and listened to the grandfather clock chiming the hour. The sound always reminded him of Arabella. He sighed. Everything reminded him of Arabella.

It was time for him to make a decision. A courier had brought a letter not more than an hour ago. He'd been ordered to send his men toward Vicksburg to attack the Federals from behind.

How could he in good conscience send his men to that hellhole? Vicksburg was a lost cause no matter how many men President Jefferson Davis insisted on sacrificing to protect it. They were too outnumbered. His handful of soldiers would be slapped down like mere mosquitoes.

He also still had sick men here to tend. They weren't coming as often, only two in the last week, but men still needed his attention, especially Charles.

Then there was Arabella. He'd vowed to himself to wait here for her no matter how long it took. If he left here, he may never see her again. Charles had said that his love had brought Ericka back to him. If that was true, then Augustus couldn't risk leaving. What if it was this house that had something to do with the time travel?

Charles had said that Ericka's brother had traveled through time in New Orleans, but his love had lived there.

He crumpled up the paper and tossed it down the stairs.

Augustus had to decide if he was willing to abandon his commission for Arabella.

CHAPTER 70

Arabella didn't bother to wipe away the tears that streamed down her cheeks. Though she'd assured Jerry that she was okay, the truth was she wasn't okay.

Seeing her fiancé had made her realize the mess her attempts at being rational and unemotional had made. She'd let herself get caught in a relationship that was not only distant, but would have been toxic if she'd stayed. As a psychologist, she considered herself a good judge of character. Now all those thoughts about herself were brought into question.

She'd opened herself up to Augustus. Had allowed herself to get emotionally close. And now here she was – hundreds of years apart from the one man she'd fallen in love with.

And now, reflecting on Jerry's statement about family, she felt all alone in the world. She had one friend at the ER, but that was a work friend. Now her only friend it seemed was the carpenter.

Annoyed with herself for thinking negative thoughts, she got up and went to look out the window. She hadn't realized it was raining. Unlike in 1863, the rain was badly needed. Grasping the curtains, she blinked. There in the trees was a movement. She squinted in the dusk at what appeared to be a man standing there looking her way. Then, just for the blink of an eye, the lawn was filled with soldiers and horses. She squeezed her eyes tightly closed, counted to three, and opened them.

All she saw were trees. Trees… and her car sitting in the circle drive.

She let the curtains fall.

Maybe Matthew was right. Maybe she was insane.

CHAPTER 71

*A*ugustus was dreaming again. About Arabella as always. But this time he dreamt she was downstairs playing the piano. Much like that first night when he'd kissed her.

He lay very still, not wanting the dream to end.

It was so very real.

Even as he felt himself coming out of the haze of sleep, the music continued. What was this? He didn't recognize the music though. Instead of the happy music she always played, this was sad, soulful music. Music that spoke to the heartache he felt with her absence.

Unable to sleep now, he tugged on his clothes, slipped into his shoes, and went downstairs.

Arabella sat at the piano. She was wearing the same dark green dress she'd been wearing the day she disappeared.

He was dreaming then. He leaned against the doorjamb and watched her. Her eyes were closed, her lips parted, and her fingers moving along the keyboard putting all the heartbreak he felt into the song. It was as though she were channeling his emotions into the music.

He barely blinked. He was afraid if he looked away, his waking dream would disappear.

CHAPTER 72

*A*rabella sat at the piano playing *Moonlight Serenade*. The sadness of the music matched the raindrops splashing against the window. Then moved into the strains of Sinatra's *All Alone*. She only played the sad songs when no one else was listening. Jerry had gone to visit his wife, reluctantly leaving her there alone. She'd assured him that she welcomed the time alone. Closing her eyes, she allowed the waves of grief and sadness to spill from her fingertips.

Almost like an accompaniment, thunder rolled in the distance, moving closer, matching the strain of the music.

She reached the end of the song, and, exhausted, dropped her hands to her lap. As the last echoes of the music drifted through the air, the clock chimed ten times.

Funny. She didn't remember winding the clock.

She opened her eyes.

And noticed the silence. Complete silence. The deafening roar of the thunder was only an echo in her head.

Then she saw him. Standing there in the doorway watching her. Augustus was everywhere she looked. Perhaps it was his ghost. She shuddered and pressed her fingers against her eyes.

She was hallucinating again. Maybe it time to go in for psychological testing. She would have to go out of state. Just for privacy's sake. She'd done some graduate work at the University of Utah Neuropsychological Institute. She'd always felt that the staff there provided the best treatment. That was where she'd go.

She slid off the bench, not the most ladylike way to maneuver her hoops, but she was alone so no harm done.

She walked around the piano, feeling like a ghost in the dark, silent house.

Yes, it was time to go in for treatment. She'd been wearing the same dress for three days, not even daring to take a shower. They'd put disheveled in the report. And disoriented to place and time. Not to mention hallucinations.

Laughter spilled from her lips. Inappropriate affect. She could write the report for them.

Careful not to trip over her skirts, she turned around, and bumped right into the solid form of what could only be a man.

CHAPTER 73

*A*ugustus was drawn to the vision sitting at the piano. When she stood up, he inched closer. The music was still in the air. A very usual dream.

Then she turned and walked right into him.

And his arms were full of Arabella.

She yelped.

"Arabella, it's me. It's Augustus."

She pulled away. "No. Ghosts aren't supposed to touch."

"I'm not a ghost, my love."

He picked her up and carried her to the sofa. He sat down with her in his lap, her arms wrapped around his neck. She shifted to adjust her hoop skirt, then she touched his face. He hadn't shaved in days. No wonder she didn't recognize him.

"It really is you," she whispered, a look of wonderment in her expression.

He chuckled. "And it really is you." He wound his fingers in her long, soft hair and pressed a kiss lightly on her lips.

She shuddered and closed her eyes, her lips trembling.

"Oh Arabella." He pressed his cheek against hers, feeling the breath from her parted lips against his skin. He wrapped his arms tightly around her. He couldn't get her close enough. "My Arabella."

She sighed against his ear and set his body on fire.

"Charles said you'd come back."

She froze. "Oh God." She disengaged herself from his hug, leaning back to search his eyes. "My father."

"Yes."

"Where is he, Augustus?" When she didn't see answers in his eyes, she shifted out of his arms, and put her feet on the floor. "I have to… Where is he?"

"He's upstairs."

She turned and gathered up her skirts.

"Wait," he said. "He isn't…" But she was gone in a whirlwind of chiffon.

CHAPTER 74

*A*rabella's feet barely touched the floor as she flew across the foyer, up the stairs, and down the hallway. As much as she wanted to see Augustus, her father's life was in peril.

Which room?

He would be in his bedroom.

She reached the door. Knocked lightly, but when there was no immediate answer, she pushed the door open. "Hello?"

No answer.

She crept forward and could see that someone was in the bed. "Father?" She whispered the word, but dread filled her heart. She was too late.

She reached the bedside and the man opened his eyes. A smile lit his lips. "Ericka."

"Father." She sat on the edge of the bed. He didn't look well. His eyes were hollow and bruised.

"I knew you'd come." He was delirious. He thought she was her mother.

She felt in her pocket for the little bottle with the antibiotics. With one hand, she unclipped the safety pin while she looked around for some water. Was there no pitcher of water in this room?

She jerked the bell cord.

Her hands trembling, she set the bottle on the nightstand. Paced to the door and back again to the bed.

His eyes had drifted closed. Oh no! She paced back to the door. Threw it open.

Villars approached, walking slowly, one hand on his back hip. "Mistress Arabella." He smiled. "It's good that you're back. Mister Charles. He needs you."

"Yes. Some water. Please. Quickly."

"Of course." He turned, picked up his pace and shuffled down the hallway.

She caught up with him in two steps. "Where is it? Let me get it."

"There's a pitcher in my room. But…"

Arabella pushed open the door at the end of the hallway and went into what was little more than a small alcove.

"It ain't fitting."

"It's okay, Villars. It's urgent."

She grabbed the glass pitcher and a glass, dashed past him, and back to her father's room.

She splashed water into the glass and took a pill from the bottle. "Charles," she said.

When he didn't respond, she put a hand behind his head. He blinked and looked at her. "Swallow this." She held the pill in front of him. He opened his mouth and she put the pill on his tongue. She held the water to his lips and he swallowed.

She sat back. Relief flooding through her. Though she had it memorized, she checked the bottle. Four times a day. She had to wait 6 hours for the next dose. In the meantime, she could clean the wound. She pulled the bottle of antiseptic out of her pocket and set it next to the pill bottle.

"What are you doing?"

She jumped. Augustus stood behind her. "I have medication."

He glanced at the 2 bottles on the nightstand. "You have Hostetter's Bitters?"

"What? No. These are… antibiotics."

"Anti what? Where did you get these?"

She bit her lip. She hadn't considered that he wouldn't understand. She thought he'd be pleased that she had a treatment for her father's condition.

"I… brought them with me."

He glanced at her sideways and picked up the bottle. "Wall Greens." He read. "Is this some new peddler of quackery? Who sold them to you?"

CHAPTER 75

"Will you help me wash his wound?"

Augustus had seen this before. Loved ones would go to any extreme to try and prolong someone's life. It was understandable, of course.

As a physician, however, it was a fine line between his patient's interest and not allowing the loved one to do more harm.

He reminded himself that Arabella was well educated. Still, the sophistication level of quackery had no doubt only grown worse with time.

"Please." Tears spilled from her eyes.

Hell, he couldn't tell her no. "Very well." He took the bottle of antiseptic from her. "How much of this do we give him?"

She looked puzzled. "Give him? No. No, this is topical. To clean the wound."

"The wound is already infected."

"But this will help. We need a cloth."

He picked up a rag from the bedside table.

She shook her head. "It has to be clean." She glanced around. "We need to boil water."

Augustus pulled the bell cord and a second later Villars pushed open the cracked door. "I have some hot water on the way, Sir."

"I'll go hurry them up." Arabella dashed from the room.

"How did you know what I wanted?" Augustus asked Villars.

Villars grinned. "I been helping Mistress Ericka for quite some time now."

Augustus sat in the chair near the bed. He picked up the smaller bottle and read the label. He attempted to open the lid, but it was locked. He held the bottle up to the lantern.

"Sir?" Villars interrupted his inspection.

"Yes, Villars?" Augustus turned to see that the older man was standing next to him.

"The Becquerel women, sir. There's something you should know."

How much did the older man know? He'd known Arabella right away. As a doctor, Augustus didn't put much stock in mysticism, but as a man, he dreaded what Villars was trying to tell him.

"They have different ways of doing things than most people."

Augustus scoffed. "Doesn't make it right."

"Sir." Villars waited for Augustus to look him in the eyes. His tone carried a weight that struck fear in Augustus' heart. "If anyone can save Mr. Charles, it's Arabella. Not you. I know you're the doctor and all, but don't fight Miss Arabella on this. I saw Mistress Ericka save Miss Andrea's life. Everyone knew she was gonna die, but she lived, Sir. Miss Andrea lived because Miss Ericka knew what to do. Let Miss Arabella save Mr. Charles." Villars turned and shuffled toward the door.

Augustus knew Villars was right. It was a hard thing to admit – that a physician's knowledge wasn't enough. That

Arabella had brought something back with her that could save this man.

He picked up the bottle and held it toward the light. There were a lot of numbers on the bottle. Numbers he'd disregarded, but as he looked more closely he noticed that one number was set apart and could easily be a date.

6.09.2018

CHAPTER 76

*A*rabella stopped on the landing and watched as Minny brought a pail of steaming hot water up the stairs.

She used the moment to take deep steadying breaths.

I need to remain calm. I'm here. I have the medication started. Everything is under control.

As Minny reached the top of the stair landing, Arabella took the pail from her hands. "I've got it from here. Thank you so much, Minny."

"I keep the hot water on all the time, so just tug the bell cord three times. I'll bring some more up to you."

"I will." Arabella smiled and turned. With both hands on the heavy water pail, she failed to lift the hem of her skirt. Instead, she stepped on her skirt and though she tried to untangle herself, it only made matters worse.

She fell onto the stairs, the pail crashing against the floor, the hot water spilling everywhere.

CHAPTER 77

*A*ugustus heard a commotion coming from the stairway.

It only took him seconds to reach the top of the stairs where he saw Arabella crumpled on the landing. He practically slid down the steps.

"Arabella!" He called her name as he gathered her into his arms, but her head lolled on in his arms. There was blood. "Oh no. No. No." In the moment, he wasn't a doctor, but a man holding his unconscious love in his arms. "Arabella." He called her name over and over.

She murmured something incomprehensible. He wiped at the blood on the side of her forehead. Her eyes blinked, but closed again.

He gathered her in his arms and carried her up the stairs to his room. As he laid her gently on his bed, she opened her eyes and looked at him. "What." She murmured.

"Arabella!"

Her eyes were glazed, but she was awake. He hugged her against his chest, but she was still limp.

He breathed in deeply and laid her back against the pillows.

I need to examine her. His heart was racing, but he went into physician mode. He needed to stop the bleeding first. He picked up a cloth from his bedside table and pressed it against the side of her head.

She blinked again and focused her gaze on his. A spurt of relief shot through him.

Her voice was soft. "Who are you?"

CHAPTER 78

$\mathcal{A}$rabella woke with a splitting headache. It was perplexing because she rarely got headaches. She opened her eyes and looked around while avoiding moving her head.

There was an adolescent girl with dark skin sitting in a chair next to her bed. The girl was humming and moving her head back and forth. Arabella didn't see any kind of phone or Ipod device… or earbuds, but the girl had a bandana wrapped around her head so maybe it just wasn't visible.

Arabella rubbed the side of her head and winced at the tenderness. Even more unexpected was she, too, was wearing some type of cloth around her head. Using both hands, she determined it was a cloth wrapped around her head, tied in the back.

Suddenly a loud bell started ringing. Arabella pressed her fingers over her ears to lessen the loud noise. It was the girl. She was ringing a handheld bell.

Seconds later, the girl stopped with the bell as a man rushed into the room. "Thank you, Leeza. You can take a break now."

He looked familiar. But she was having trouble focusing

with all the noise and the headache. He smelled good. Like soap
and antiseptic. It reminded her of something… A hospital. Was
she in a hospital?

"Arabella."

Yes. She blinked and gazed into the man's deep blue eyes.
His handsome face was lined with worry.

"Do you know who I am?"

She felt like she should know him. "You're my doctor?"

He scrunched his brows. "Yes… Do you know my name?"

She couldn't think. She shook her head, but immediately
stopped when it made her head hurt worse.

She put her hand on the bandage wrapped around her head.
"What is this?"

"It's a bandage. You fell. And hit your head."

"When?"

"A day and half ago."

She licked her dry lips. "Water."

He put a glass to her lips and she sipped. The water tasted
different. It was warm.

"How do you feel?"

"My head is pounding."

"You hit your head."

"Where?"

"On the stairs. You tripped over your dress."

How did someone trip over their dress? She hadn't worn a
long dress since senior prom. "How is that even possible?"

He seemed confused by her question. "The skirt…" He
placed a wrist on her forehead. "No fever," he murmured. She
closed her eyes again. His voice was soothing. Familiar even.

"Do you have any Tylenol?

"I don't think so."

CHAPTER 79

Augustus checked his watch. He'd been giving Charles the medicine every six hours. The bottle said four a day, so he figured that was the safest way to do it.

After listening to what Villars had to say, Augustus had decided not to discount Charles' ramblings after all. They both seemed to think that the Becquerel women had magical healing powers.

As Charles began to recover, Augustus became less inclined to argue.

He had another two hours before he had to give Charles his dose. Arabella was asleep again. He felt better that she had least regained consciousness, even if she didn't seem to know who he was or even where she was. More specifically, she didn't seem to know *when* she was.

He'd had one of the women undress her and put a nightgown on her. He folded back the blanket and climbed into bed next to her.

Maybe if he just held her, snuggled her close against him, it would help her heal. He had no reason to believe that this was a rational idea, but with all that he'd seen lately, he was inclined to believe just about anything.

He cushioned her head with his arm and snuggled behind her back. She backed against him, fitting herself perfectly against him. As much time as they'd spent together, they'd never lain in a bed together. Augustus hadn't done anything that could tarnish her reputation. But now, that no longer seemed important. He wanted to seize every moment to be close to her, no matter the consequences.

He'd let the girls get her undressed and into her nightgown. But he'd carefully wrapped a bandage around her head to stop the bleeding just over her right eye. He made sure the cloths were clean, just as he had seen her do.

Other than that, he'd been helpless. She'd regained consciousness a couple of times, but she didn't seem to know him or even to know herself.

He read about cases where people with head trauma never woke up. Minny had watched helplessly as she'd tripped over her own skirts and had fallen on the stairs. Fortunately, she'd been standing on the landing and had fallen up, not down. Things could have been a lot worse, though right now, he was having a hard time being optimistic.

She was the woman he wanted to live the rest of his life with. But now she was comatose and he was helpless to do anything about it. Even as a doctor he was helpless.

The only thing he could do was to hold her. To hold her and to make sure that when she did wake, and she would wake - she had to - that he had kept her father alive.

CHAPTER 80

*A*rabella woke from a dream so vivid she turned over and ran a hand over the empty space on the bed behind her. She sat up and looked around her. It was completely dark other than a little sliver of moonlight coming in through the closed curtains.

At first she couldn't place where she was, but she recognized the huge four-poster bed she was in the middle of and the bureau on the other side of the room.

She was in the plantation house left to her by her great-grandmother. She had a vague memory of coming here to learn more about this place and then being swept back to 1863.

1863.

It must be 1863 then because Jerry had the room in a state of disarray with his remodeling.

She lay back down hugging the extra pillow to her, and breathed in its manly scent.

Augustus.

A jumble of memories came back in a rush. Augustus smiling at her across the top of the piano. Augustus picking her up. Kissing her lips. Hours of conversation. Tending wounded soldiers. He did the medical part and she listened to them talk.

Wounded soldiers. Bullet wounds.

Amputations.

Charles Becquerel.

Her father.

Died June 12, 1863.

From infection resulting from leg amputation.

She threw the blankets off and slid off the edge of the bed. What was the date? Was she too late?

Where were her clothes? She was wearing a nightgown. *How had that happened?*

She'd brought medicine with her in her dress pockets. Augustus' words played in her head. *Hostetter's Bitters. Quackery.* There hadn't been time to convince him that the medicine could save her father's life.

She glanced around, but it was dark. She didn't have time to search for anything to wear.

She padded to the door in her bare feet and her nightgown and threw the door open. The hallway was empty and the house was quiet. She didn't know what time it was, but she could hear the ticking of the grandfather clock drifting from downstairs.

She reached the door of her father's bedroom and knocked. No answer. She knocked louder.

She pushed the door open. "Father?" She stepped through the threshold and searched for him in the bed.

Even in the darkness, she could see that the bed was neatly made. A quick glance told her that no one was in the room.

No!

Her hand still on the doorknob, she fell to her knees.

I'm too late.

CHAPTER 81

*A*ugustus puffed smoke from the cigar that Charles had found hidden away in his study. He'd been impressed by Charles' skills at hiding things in plain view. He'd pulled the cigars from the inside of a hollowed out book from his bookshelf.

"Did you always know you wanted to be a doctor?" Charles asked, his leg propped on the railing of the front porch.

"Surely you jest. I was raised on a plantation, not much different from this one. I thought I'd grow up to be a farmer."

"What changed your mind?"

"Besides the war?" Augustus shrugged. "Times changes. My father freed his slaves years ago at the first hint of our country changing."

"Sounds like he was a man ahead of his time."

"He was. He was one of the most proactive men I've ever known."

"Is he fighting?"

"My father? No. He passed away from a heart attack when I was sixteen years old." Augustus blew a smoke ring into the air. "That was probably when I first decided to study medicine. I remember my mother sent for a doctor, but the only person who would come out that far on that morning was a quack. I remember thinking that there should be more doctors."

"That must have been a difficult time."

Augustus scoffed. "You sound like Arabella. But, yes, it was difficult." He watched his friend. Charles appeared to be in full recovery. "Do you plan to return to the army?"

"What? No. The war is a lost cause and the time has come for me to take care of my own."

"I agree. I've been granted leave from the army."

"That's good news then. But you'll be staying on here?"

"Of course." Augustus blew a smoke ring. In truth he had many things to contemplate. Arabella was a confounding variable in any plans he was considering. He chose, however, not to voice these concerns to Charles.

After the clock chimed eight times, Augustus pulled a little medicine bottle from his pocket, uncorked it, and handed Charles a pill. It wasn't the original pill bottle. He'd broken that one trying to get it open. It was tucked away in his trunk. But Augustus had the instructions memorized and he watched the time like a hawk to make sure Charles didn't miss a dose.

At the mention of Arabella, he grew restless. Although he enjoyed Charles' company, he checked on Arabella every hour. And had spent countless hours over the last two days holding her, willing her to wake up. To wake up and know who he was.

She had his heart and this injury was unbearable, leaving him hanging by a thread. He'd gotten caught up in a few things and then Charles wanted to smoke a cigar, so it had been a few hours since he'd checked on Arabella. He grew restless.

He stood up. "I appreciate the fine cigar, my friend, but..."

Charles grinned. "But it's time to check on my daughter."

"With your blessing, Sir." He knew Charles would give it and he knew that even if he didn't he wouldn't stay away from Arabella.

Just as he'd expected, Charles waved him off. "It's good to be out of that bed. I've been relegated to it far too long."

"Shall I help you back to your room?"

"No. Go ahead. I'll get back."

"I'll make sure someone comes for you soon."

"Please. Don't hurry. I'm enjoying the fresh air."

Augustus went into the house and raced up the stairs. He heard several people talking at once.

Then his stomach dropped when he saw someone kneeling on the floor. He'd been away too long.

Just as he neared them, he watched as Villars helped Arabella to her feet.

When she saw Augustus, she ran toward him. "Augustus." Her eyes filled with tears as she took his arm and gazed up at him. Her fingertips dug into his arm.

"How could you let my father die?"

CHAPTER 82

Augustus went to Arabella, but she turned away, a hand over her eyes. "I brought medicine."

"You did. Arabella." He put a hand on her shoulder. When she didn't pull away, he pulled her against him into a hug. "Arabella. The medicine. It worked."

She grew very still. Then slowly lifted her chin and looked into his eyes. "It worked? But?" She glanced toward the bedroom.

Augustus smiled. "Your father is downstairs. On the veranda."

"Are you sure?"

"Of course. I just left him. He wanted some fresh air."

"I thought…" She turned her back to him, went to the banister and put her hands on the rail. He stood silently, counting the seconds. Waiting.

"What happened?"

"You tripped on your skirts and fell. You hit your head on the stairs."

"I don't remember." She shook her head.

"You had amnesia."

"It was you? You took care of me?"

"I sat with you for hours." He didn't tell her about the hours he spent lying with her, holding her close, willing her to regain consciousness.

"I just slept the whole time?"

"Pretty much. There wasn't really anything I could do." He wanted to tell how he feared she would never wake up. How he thought she'd been lost to him forever, but she needed time to orient herself.

She turned back to face him. "How long was I out?"

"Three days."

She looked down, ran her hands over her nightgown. He followed her gaze and noticed for the first time the sheerness of her gown. She seemed to notice is also as her face flushed with a lovely rose color. "I should… um. I'm not dressed properly."

Augustus took off his coat and helped her put her arms through the sleeves. It was far too big for her. He rolled the sleeves up so that her hands were free.

He pulled the lapels together. "There."

Her lashes fluttered and he looked into her mesmerizing green eyes. Her lips parted and he wanted so much to kiss her. To taste her full lips again.

But she was vulnerable and he held back, kissing her on the forehead instead.

He put his arms around her and held her head against his chest.

CHAPTER 83

*A*rabella was enveloped in Augustus' scent. His manly scent. Her arms went around him and she held on. She couldn't get close enough to him. His jacket was long, covering her to her knees. It was surprisingly heavy. How did he wear this all day long without becoming exhausted?

"You should sit." Her eyes fluttered open. He released her and took her hand. They took two steps toward her bedroom.

"Arabella?"

She turned and saw Charles standing there only a few feet away, supporting his weight with a cane. He appeared to have both his legs. Relief flashed through her and her eyes welled with tears. "Father." Her voice caught in her throat.

Charles grinned and held out his free arm.

Arabella closed the distance between them and threw her arms around her father. *Family.* She had family. She turned and smiled at Augustus, tears spilling from her eyes.

Augustus nodded, then turned and walked down the hall toward his room.

"Arabella." Charles held her elbow. "My God." He

swallowed, then whispered. "You look so much like your mother."

"Vaughn said the same thing."

"Vaughn. She raised you?"

"Yes." Arabella's smile turned upside down. "She passed away about a month ago."

"Oh, I hate to hear that. Ericka will, too. Vaughn was a good mother then?"

"She was the best. And Jonathan."

"I'm sorry," he said, wobbling.

"No." She took his arm. "Let's sit."

"I'm so much better." He sat in a chair just inside his bedroom door. She sat next to him. "And I understand I have you to thank for that."

"I um… I don't know how much you know."

He grinned. "I know all about the time travel."

Arabella leaned forward. "I have so many questions. So many unanswered questions now that I'm here. Now that I've found you."

CHAPTER 84

$\mathcal{A}$ugustus climbed into bed and stared at the ceiling. He'd left Arabella with her father. They had a lot of catching up to do and he didn't want to intrude.

Plus, he needed to think.

She'd been quick to think that he'd let her father die.

He shouldn't blame her. He hadn't exactly welcomed her treatment methods.

But the medicine had worked. It was like a miracle drug. If he could get his hands on some of that... But all good things must come in time.

It had occurred to him that perhaps she didn't feel the same way about him.

Now that she'd saved her father's life, she'd want to get back to her own time.

And rightly so. In her time, there was no need for amputations. There was medication to bring a man back from the brink of death.

He could only think and hope that if he truly loved her, he would want her to go back to her own time. A time when she could be safe.

He wasn't able to provide the things she was accustomed to. He couldn't even help her wake from a coma.

If he loved her, he had to let her go.

CHAPTER 85

"So." Charles was saying. "We figured out that something had happened and Vaughn had taken you with her."

"That must have been awful for you."

"It was heartbreaking. But we kept thinking she would come back. That she'd somehow find a way to get you back."

"She never told me about the time travel. She never even told me about this house. She left it to me in her will. The first night I was here I came back to 1863."

"And you stayed?"

"Yes, until the other day when you came home."

"Ericka went back and forth several times before she stayed." He sipped his brandy and leaned back in his chair. "I wonder why Vaughn kept you from us."

"I think she left a letter for me, but the ink got smudged and I wasn't able to read it."

"That's too bad."

"That might be an understatement."

"So tell me about your life in the future. How do you spend your days?"

"I um... I listen to people talk about things that are bothering them."

CHAPTER 86

When Arabella woke the next morning, the birds were already up. She'd stayed up late talking with her father. They'd had so many things to talk about. It had been a relief to have someone to talk to who understood enough about her life in the future to follow and… someone who didn't think she needed to go to the insane asylum.

Her father. It was still surreal to think about talking with the father she'd grown up thinking had died when she was an infant. How often as a child had she wished for just one conversation with him?

The only thing missing had been Augustus.

When she'd asked Charles about him, he'd shrugged it off, saying that Augustus was merely giving them some privacy.

After washing her face, she dressed for the day. It would be a good day for a bath. She missed the daily showers she was accustomed to. At the most, she could go every other day.

She went to sit at the vanity and began brushing her hair.

It was then that she noticed a folded piece of paper tucked into the side of the mirror between the glass and the wood frame. She'd almost overlooked it. Wondering how long it had been there, she pulled it loose and with a feeling a dread unfolded it.

My Dearest Arabella,

You'll wonder why I wrote you instead of speaking to you of this in person. The truth is I couldn't bear to say good-bye. I've received permission to resign from the army and I must go home. I've received no communication from my mother and sisters in several months and I fear for their safety. Now that your father is well, I feel safe in leaving you in his care.

Yours truly,

Augustus

Arabella reread the letter. She hadn't seen Augustus since last evening when she'd been reunited with her father. Though she replayed the conversation over in her head, she couldn't recall anything out of the ordinary other than Augustus walking off. Her father had assured her it was of no concern. In truth, she'd been so focused on Charles, that she'd barely noticed Augustus at that point.

CHAPTER 87

*A*ugustus stood in the center of what had been his family's plantation home and used a sturdy tree limb to search through the charred rubble. His heart was in his throat. He didn't know if his mother and two sisters had survived the fire.

He reached down and picked up a silver heart-shaped locket covered in soot and wiped it on his sleeve. He recognized it as one his mother wore. In fact, he rarely saw her without it. Using his fingernail, he opened the little locket door to reveal a likeness of his mother and father. They had been so young when they'd sat for the photograph. Probably even before Augustus was born.

His mother wouldn't leave this locket on purpose. His throat clutched as his mind raced at the dire possibilities that could have happened to his family.

He prayed to God that they weren't in the fire.

A few minutes later, he saw his neighbor walking down his drive. Old Mr. Kenneth must be nearing ninety years old, but got around better than a lot of people half his age. In fact, Kenneth was the oldest person Augustus had ever met.

He waved as he neared Augustus. "I saw you come in on what's left of that horse."

Augustus would have smiled, but his heart was too heavy. Kenneth could keep his sense of humor through anything. "What happened here?"

"Yankees."

One word explained it all. Augustus lifted his hat and ran a hand through his hair. "My mother? My sisters?" Even as he asked, he dreaded the worst.

"The Yankees run 'em off before they set fire to it."

Augustus heaved a sigh of relief that almost took him to his knees. He had barely been able to take a breath from the moment he rounded the corner and saw the house burned to the ground, nothing left but the spiral staircase in the middle.

"I've been watching for you," Kenneth added. "The last thing I wanted was for you or your brother to come back here and find the place like this."

"Where are they?"

"We set up a little refugee camp of sorts behind my house." He looked apologetic. "You know I would have taken them in the house, but me and my wife don't have the room."

"Don't apologize Kenneth. I appreciate you looking out for them."

"They've been a wonderful help. Did you know that Allison can make an apple pie that's the best in the county?"

"I did. I've missed her cooking." Allison may not could hold a tune on the piano, but she could bake like nobody else.

"Come on." Kenneth put an arm around his shoulder. "They'll be ecstatic to see you."

Augustus slipped the little locket in his pocket, grabbed his horse's reins and began the half mile long walk to his neighbor's house.

CHAPTER 88

"What happened while I was out?" Arabella paced from the side of Charles's study to the window and back again. She kept her skirt fisted in one hand, careful not to trip over it again.

"Nothing. He gave me that medicine you brought with you and cleaned my wound until I healed enough to get out of bed."

"Hmm." She stood at the window staring down the driveway. It just didn't add up. He'd taken care of both of them. But he was a doctor. He had no reason to be overwhelmed. "Are you certain he didn't say anything to you that suggested he might be leaving?"

"I'm certain. In fact, he told me that he was granted an army retirement and was planning to stay here."

"He got a letter?"

"I suppose so, yes."

Perhaps he'd received some other correspondence. Orders? Not if he was granted retirement. "It doesn't add up," she muttered.

Charles came to stand next to her. "Sometimes men do

things that don't make any sense at the time. Sometimes it makes sense later. Sometimes not."

Arabella chuckled. "That's true of everyone." She turned and faced her father. "Do you think he'll be back?"

"I don't know ma petite cherie."

She sighed. In her quest to save her father's life, had she somehow offended Augustus?

Suddenly she vaguely recalled the words she'd spoken to him the moment she'd seen him after waking up from her head injury. *How could you let my father die?*

CHAPTER 89

"*I* think I messed up."

Arabella sat on the sofa in the parlor. Her father sat in a chair, reading. They'd had dinner - cornbread and peas just before the sun started its downward trend toward the horizon.

Charles looked up from his book. "What could you possibly have done?"

"I think…" The thoughts were still a bit scattered, not quite full-formed. "I might have not given Augustus enough attention and that's why he left." She spat the words out, as though getting them out there somehow made it easier.

"Nonsense." Where did that come from?"

"I accused him of letting you die."

"You didn't know."

"But that's not the most affectionate way to tell someone how much you missed them."

Charles laughed. "I can assure you that men don't think that way."

"How do you know?" She said, then bit her lip when he looked at her sideways.

"You're still trying to figure out why he left."

"I feel like I took him for granted or something."

Charles set his book aside. "Arabella." He waited until she tilted her head to look him in the eyes. "It's not something you did."

"How do you know that?"

"Because I'm a man. It's natural for daughters to worry about their fathers. You and Augustus saved my life. You for bringing the medicine to me and him for administering it when you couldn't. It looks to me like the two of you are a good pair."

Arabella closed her eyes and listened to the frogs and crickets outside the open window. She understood what Charles was saying. And she knew that all things being equal he was right.

But he had failed to take into consideration one small detail. If her father was right and love was the driving force that brought Becquerel women back in time, and Augustus had left, why was she still here?

Why hadn't she returned to her own time?

CHAPTER 90

Three Weeks Later

Morale was low as Vicksburg struggled to stay alive against the relentless siege from the Northerners. Word must have spread quickly that the Becquerels no longer had a physician – only a couple of stragglers appeared at their doorstep and they weren't physically wounded, but rather starving and exhausted.

Arabella wandered the halls, taking care of things as needed. She learned to make candles and to make coffee out of sweet potatoes.

Times were hard.

They hadn't received word from Ericka, but with the battles being fought around them, both Arabella and Charles hoped she had ignored his letters and stayed safely in New Orleans.

Folding her freshly washed and dried garments and placing them in the armoire, Arabella's hand brushed against her cell phone. She hadn't even thought about a cell phone in days.

She curled up on the settee in her room and switched on

the power. It was almost a shock to see the little screen light up. Even though she checked, there was, of course, no service.

She tapped on the photos and scrolled through to the picture she'd taken of Augustus. She ran a finger lightly against the image of his face and felt her heart tug.

Despite what her father said, her gut told her that she had somehow let Augustus down. They had been attached at the hip before she'd gone back to her time.

Perhaps that was it. Perhaps it wasn't so much that she hadn't paid enough attention to him, but rather he was freaked out by the idea that she was from the future.

She had, after all, disappeared in front of his eyes. Most people would find that disconcerting to say the least.

She tried to put herself in his shoes. Would she want to be in a relationship with someone who could disappear with no warning supposedly to go to the future?

Who knows?

It just doesn't add up.

He already knew she was from the future before she disappeared. The idea of going after him had crossed her mind a few times, but the thought of going out on foot or even on a horse in the middle of a war torn country, made her feel sick to her stomach.

Besides, he was the one who left, so if he'd wanted to be with her, he would have stayed. Or at least talked to her about where he was going and when he would be back.

She sighed and closed her phone. She was missing something, but she couldn't sort it out. Only he could provide the missing piece.

And she couldn't help but think that in her modern day terms, she'd been dumped. And if that were the case, then it really didn't matter what the reason was.

CHAPTER 91

It was raining again. Augustus couldn't remember ever seeing so much rain day after day after day.

He stood pressed against the side of a gully with his mother and his two sisters. They didn't have a horse, so they were on foot.

"Don't make a sound." He whispered, thankful that the rain would help muffle any inadvertent sounds. Unfortunately, the rain would keep the soldiers' eyes down. And looking down was the last thing he needed them to do.

They were Yankees. He could tell by the sound of their horses. It was something he couldn't explain, but a well-outfitted and well-fed horse walked differently than an emaciated horse. Even if he merely imagined it, he'd never been wrong.

As the first horse and rider crossed the path above them, he knew he was right. "Watch out for the gully on your right."

Damn. Now they'd all be looking at the gully. And going to a Yankee prison would not do anything to help his family to safety. Though he could barely see through the rain running through his eyes, he kept his eyes open. His fingers were wrapped tightly around the pistol beneath his coat.

The women were crouched on the ground, pressed against the side of the gully, their heads down.

Horse after horse passed by inches above them. If only one soldier happened to catch a glimpse of one of them, they would be on them like flies. He'd be no match against the regiment, no matter how small. And he was well aware of what happened to women traveling alone. There were true gentlemen out there, but there were also scoundrels and worse.

He needed to lower his head, to let the brim of his hat divert the rain out of his eyes, but he didn't dare move a muscle. Any movement could alert the soldiers to their presence.

He held his breath when one of the horses stopped just above them. "Hey Leonard, whatcha stopping for?"

"I need to take a piss."

"In the rain?"

"Ha." The soldier called Leonard shifted in his saddle. Augustus held his breath. And hoped like hell that his sisters didn't notice the stream of piss mixed with rainwater falling over their heads. "When did that matter?"

"Do you see that?" Leonard asked.

Augustus tightened his hold on his pistol. Braced himself for battle.

"What?" The other soldier called out from behind.

"I saw something. Hold up."

A musket shot rang out above his head. One of the women shrieked.

CHAPTER 92

"Father, I need to talk to you."

Charles pushed aside his ledger and set his quill aside. "Here." He came around his desk and sat at one of the two chairs in front of the fireplace. He gestured for her to sit in the other. "What's troubling you?"

She couldn't help but smile at how naturally he invited her to sit and talk. Maybe she'd inherited the gene that made her a psychologist from him.

"I think I should go home." She'd worried over this for weeks. It just seemed logical. She had nothing productive to do here. At least at home – in her time – she had a career.

"Home." He nodded.

He knew what she meant by that. She could see the disappointment in his expression. She rushed to explain. "I like being here, with you, but I don't belong here. I don't have anything to do."

"You can do anything you want to do."

"You know what I mean. I don't have a career – a profession – here. At home I work with people to help them feel better."

"You can do that here."

She blew out a breath. "It's not something people do… yet."

"There's nothing wrong with being the first to do something."

"I can't just change the course of history." *But… who would know…*

"The war can't go on forever. Things should get better."

From what she'd learned in history, things would get a lot worse before they would get better, with reconstruction going on for years. But she didn't tell him that. There was no need. The truth was she could barely stand to be here without Augustus. Everything reminded her of him. Her eyes welled with tears and she turned her head away so Charles couldn't see.

"Arabella." Charles' voice was soft.

Her breath hitched as the tears started to fall. She put a hand over her eyes. *I won't cry.*

"This is about Augustus?"

She nodded.

"I don't understand it either. I wish your mother were here. She'd know what to do."

"I just want to go home."

CHAPTER 93

irt splashed over their heads as the horses moved away from them.

Silence.

Augustus waited. Lowered his head enough to shield his eyes from the rain. He counted to ten.

Then he slid down to the ground.

This war was going to be the death of him yet.

He heard voices in the distance as the echo from the gunshot faded. The Yankees, it seemed, had shot themselves a rabbit.

Adeline touched his shoulder and whispered. "I think we can move now."

Augustus nodded. "Let's give them a minute to make sure they're out of earshot. He breathed out a ragged breath. Did his family know just how close they'd come to disaster? He hoped not.

Ten minutes passed before the silence returned to normal. Birdsong filled the trees again.

"Augustus." His mother held out her hand for him to help her up. "Will this war never end?"

"It can't end soon enough."

Their skirts were caked with mud, but their jaws were set with resolve.

Women truly were the heroes of this war.

CHAPTER 94

*A*rabella spent the next day rummaging in the attic. She searched every trunk and every wooden box she could find.

She just needed some clue. Some direction. Something to point her in the right direction about how to get home. So far she'd found nothing but old clothing, ribbons, a jewelry box full of jewelry, and some toys. Typical things for an attic.

The light was waning, so she shoved aside the box she'd just been rummaging through. There was a small valise that she hadn't noticed before. The black leather was weathered and cracked. She picked it up. It was fairly light, but not light enough to be empty.

She took it with her back to her room and lit the kerosene lantern.

With enough light now, she snapped open the valise and pulled out yards and yards of white material – discolored now with age.

A dress.

She laid the dress out on the bed, carefully arranging the lace and ruffles.

It was a dress she'd seen in pictures. Countless times.
The dress belonged to Vaughn.
It was Vaughn's wedding dress.

CHAPTER 95

Augustus brought in the last box from the wagon. His mother and two sisters had spent some time in town replacing some of the things that had been lost in the fire. Despite slim pickings, they'd managed to replace most of their necessities. Even though they'd lost everything but the clothes on their backs, thank God they'd been allowed to get out before the fire.

He'd brought them to Natchez and found a house for room and board. He could just as well have taken them to Jackson. Vicksburg was out of the question, of course, with the siege in full force. He could only imagine the horrid conditions they must be enduring there – both soldiers and civilians alike. It was a wonder he and his family had been allowed to move about the country as easily as they had.

"What are you going to do now?" Allison asked.

His youngest sister was the prettiest of the two. He loved them equally, but she had gotten the beauty. His other sister was smarter. But still sometimes Allison was more perceptive than Adeline.

"I'm going to find us something to eat."

"No. Silly. I mean what are you going to do about the girl."

Augustus hadn't said anything to his family about Arabella. He hadn't even alluded to her existence. "I don't know what you mean."

"I haven't seen you this downcast since little Mary Lou moved away when we were children."

"It's the war," he said automatically. The war took the blame for everything. Rightly so. Especially since he didn't have time to formulate a plausible reason why she was wrong when she was ever so right.

Allison rolled her eyes. "I'm your sister. You can tell me anything."

Augustus crossed his arms, leaned back against the door, and studied his sister. She was a woman now – not the little girl running around in short dresses. Maybe a woman would understand. "Very well."

She smiled smugly.

"I met a girl from… the city."

Allison lifted an eyebrow. "Go on."

"I thought she was going to stay around, but she left."

"Why?"

"I'm not sure. But she came back."

"That's what you wanted, right?"

"It was. But I could see that she was a city girl and I couldn't imagine why she would stay around when she could go back to the city anytime."

"So…? You left?"

"Yes." He was rather pleased with himself for finding a way to tell his sister everything without actually telling her anything.

"Gus." She glared at him. "Please tell me why men are so daft."

"You're insulting me now." She was the only one allowed to call him Gus.

"I'm trying to make you see. You're walking around all mopey. And you're the one who created the problem."

I should have known better than to tell her. "It's not that simple."

"She's married then?"

"No. Of course not."

"Betrothed?"

"We never talked about it."

She made a face. "But you love her?"

His breath hitched in his throat. "Yes." He breathed.

She scowled. "Why do people always try to make love difficult?"

He shrugged.

"So you love her, but she doesn't know it. And obviously you never talked about it."

"The war…"

"Nonsense. This has nothing to do with the war. You can't blame male stupidity on the war."

CHAPTER 96

*A*rabella opened her bedroom door. Villars stood there with a plate of food and a pitcher of water on a rolling cart.

"I'm sorry to disturb you, Miss Arabella, but Mr. Charles said you didn't come down for supper and since you spent the day in the attic, I thought you might be hungry."

Arabella smiled and stepped aside for Villars to push the cart into the room. He had the art of vagueness down to a science. He hadn't said whether he or her father had thought to bring her food.

He took the plate and pitcher from the cart, setting them on the little table. "Will you be needing anything else?"

Arabella had her back to him, her attention on the dress.

"Where did you find Miss Vaughn's wedding dress?"

"In the attic. You recognize it then?"

"Of course." Villars started to say more, but closed his mouth and waited.

"Villars." Arabella had searched the house and learned everything her father could tell her about her mother and great-grandmother and time travel. Unfortunately, it wasn't enough. But Villars knew everything and saw everything that happened in this house. Here was an untapped resource standing in front of her.

"Yes ma'am."

"What do you know about time travel?"

CHAPTER 97

Augustus walked through the woods behind the house he and his family had just moved into. He missed walking through the cotton fields back home. He'd discovered a long time ago that taking a walk in the fresh air cleared his mind. It was especially helpful when needed to sort something out.

And right now he had some serious sorting to do.

Allison's words haunted him. Was he being an idiot?

He'd thought he'd made the right choice in leaving Arabella.

He'd been right to go to his family and get them to safety. He had no regrets there. But leaving Arabella the way he had, with no explanation other than a simple note... Perhaps that had been a bad decision.

He'd made the choice in haste. He rarely did anything important without thinking it through first. And Arabella was important.

He couldn't stop thinking about her. And his heart ached from missing her. The thought of never seeing her again was making him physically ill.

He'd heard of people dying from a broken heart, but as a

physician he'd never put much stock in it. But now… he may be dying of a broken heart himself.

And the whole thing was his doing.

But it was so much more complicated than his sister could fathom. It wasn't just a matter of telling her how he felt and living happily ever after. It was a matter of doing what was best for Arabella. What was best for the woman he loved.

She was from a different time. A better time. A time where taking pills could cure a man's infected limb so that an amputation wasn't necessary.

Augustus hadn't realized he'd reached the Mississippi. He sat down on the bluff and watched the muddy water flowing past.

The water snagged tiny pieces of silt as it flowed past, taking the silt with it. Just as seconds were carried away by minutes and minutes by hours. Seconds went unnoticed, but then so many passed that life was over.

He looked downriver toward the Becquerel estate. He was so close to her, yet so far. What would she do if given the choice? Would she remain here with her parents in the middle of this ungodly war or would she go back to the future?

If given a choice.

Charles believed that love was the thing that had brought her here.

Without Augustus, she was free to do whatever she wanted.

She could travel back to the future where medicine could save lives and likenesses could be captured on a mirrored device. What wonders the future must hold.

No. He'd made the right decision.

She needed to be free to find a way home.

CHAPTER 98

Villars' eyes widened and he took a step back. "Oh no, Miss. It ain't fitting for me to be talking about such things with you."

Arabella's heartbeat quickened. "Then you do know something."

"I can't say anything. No ma'am." He took a step back.

Arabella put her hands on her hips. "Villars. You're not afraid?"

Villars froze and stood up straight. "Yes ma'am." His chin quivered just a little.

Arabella tilted her head to the side. "I understand. Come." She gestured toward the little sitting area. "Let's sit for a minute."

"Miss Arabella. It ain't proper."

"Nonsense. You've been part of this family your whole life."

Villars took a step forward, his eyes wide.

Arabella sat and patted the seat of the chair across from her. He didn't move. "I need your help with something."

Using his cane for support, Villars sat across from her.

"Thank you." Arabella smiled.

"It ain't fitting, but I'd do anything for this family."

"I believe that." She locked her hands together in her lap. She hadn't considered that Villars would be reluctant to talk with her. "It must have been quite a shock for you to see me that first time."

"Oh yes ma'am. You was just a baby, but you're the spitting image of Missus Ericka. I mean you look just like she did. It was like seeing her young again."

Arabella nodded. "You knew."

"I been expected you to come back but it's been longer than anyone ever thought."

"It has been a long time."

Villars seemed a little more comfortable now. He took off his hat and balanced it on his knees. "What do you want to know?"

"It seems random – the time travel. It seems to just happen without warning. What do you think makes it happen?"

He kept his dark brown eyes trained on her as he seemed to consider. "You're wanting to go back to your time."

"I might." She admitted.

"It will break Missus Ericka's heart."

"I'm just trying to understand."

Villars slowly blew out his breath. "I don't think nobody really knows." He said softly.

"But you do."

He nodded. "It happens when the sky splits. Just like the legend says."

"What do you mean the sky splits?"

"It's the thunderstorms."

CHAPTER 99

Augustus sat next to the bed of a child burning with fever. He hadn't decided what he wanted to do next, but his mother had told their new neighbors that he was a physician and they had told their friends and word had traveled.

So here he sat. Helpless.

The child was under a heap of wool blankets, but still shivered with a vengeance.

Augustus had no quinine to alleviate her suffering. The girl was already delusional and didn't even know her own mother.

He was helpless. He could hear the girl's mother in the other room, weeping. She'd lost her son at Bull Run from dysentery.

Now she would lose her daughter. Both her children lost to disease.

Augustus put a hand on the girl's forehead. The heat nearly scorched his skin. What good was he as a doctor? He lost more patients than he helped. *It's the war.*

But this girl would die and she had nothing to do with the war.

She'd die because he couldn't help her.

Perhaps there was a better place somewhere that he could practice medicine.

Not a better place so much, but a better time.

CHAPTER 100

Arabella sat in her sitting room staring out the window. She'd slid the chair over and sat holding her cell phone. In the movie Somewhere in Time, Christopher Reeve had gone forward in time just by seeing a modern day coin. Maybe if she held her cell phone, the same would happen to her.

It was just a movie.

It was make believe. But this. This was real.

And holding her cell phone, looking at picture of cars and airplanes didn't change anything.

Thunderstorms.

Villars firmly believed that time travel occurred during thunderstorms. *When the skies split open.*

Lightening, Arabella supposed was what he referred to as the sky splitting. As far-fetched as it sounded, there had been a thunderstorm all three times she'd travelled through time. She'd hardly even noticed. But now, she wondered if he had it figured out.

He hadn't been able to further explain the legend he referred to, except something about a rip in time.

She squinted against the sunlight streaming through the window. It was a cloudless summer day with no storms in sight.

She had no weather channel to check.

Discouraged, she took her phone back and hid it on a shelf in her wardrobe beneath a blue chiffon dress.

If it had been storming every time Arabella had gone through time and Villars claimed that both Ericka and Vaughn travelled when it was storming, his belief was plausible.

Yet… there was still that missing piece. Was it the house? Or the grandfather clock?

She wandered downstairs and stood in front of the ticking clock. She'd been told it usually happened here. It had always happened right here for her – even as an infant being held in Vaughn's arms.

Perhaps it was a combination of things. She glanced outside at the glaring sunlight. Someone had left the door open to catch whatever stray breeze happened by. If thunder truly was required, it looked like it was going to be quite some time before she could test it out.

She slapped a mosquito on her arm, smearing blood all over her hand.

CHAPTER 101

Augustus spurred the horse—the horse he now knew why he got at such good price for—down the drive toward the Becquerel estate. The horse had done well, but the old fellow didn't have much left in him.

Now that Augustus had made his decision, he was ready to implement his plan.

The house was quiet. It appeared to be deserted even. He dismounted in front of the house and sprinted up the stairs. Had something happened while he was gone? The Yankees perhaps? He rapped on the door. Waited. But no one answered. Gone were the days of butlers.

He rapped on the door again, then went back down the front steps and picked his way around the house to the back. His soldiers had gone, leaving the grounds deserted.

As he walked around the side of the house, he heard voices in a heated discussion. Slowing, he stopped at the back corner and listened.

He recognized Charles' voice, but not the other man.

"You sent for them?"

"Yes. I thought I was going to die." Charles spoke quietly and calmly.

"How did you expect them to make their way across the country in the middle of a damn war?"

"I don't know. I trusted Ericka to come if she could."

The other man scoffed. "Of course she would try. No matter if it was safe or not. And Camille would follow at her heels."

Camille. Ericka's sister-in-law if Augustus remembered correctly. Then this must be Ericka's brother, Bradley.

Bradley was also from the future.

"They didn't come, so they must have decided it was best to stay put." Charles said.

"But you don't know that. You said you haven't heard from them."

"I have not."

"Not even a word." Bradley bit out the words.

Charles was silent.

"I have to go find them."

"Find them how?"

"How the hell should I know? I can't just sit here. And do nothing."

"Go then."

Augustus heard the weariness in Charles' voice.

"I'll leave first thing in the morning." Footsteps. Then the door slammed.

Augustus waited a beat, then went around the house so Charles could see him.

"Augustus!" Charles cried "Thank God you're here."

"What's wrong?" Augustus felt his heart rate quicken at his friend's troubled expression.

"It's Arabella."

CHAPTER 102

rabella shoved the blanket off of her.

Again.

She was shivering and someone kept covering her up. It would make sense, of course, except that she'd spent enough time in hospitals to know that it only made a fever worse. When she pointed this out to them, they shook their heads and called her addled.

She'd asked for mosquito netting, but none could be found. Apparently, the soldiers had somehow managed to take it with them. So she stayed under a sheet and did the best she could to avoid further mosquito bites.

Charles had asked for quinine, but none of that could be found either.

The war.

The war left them with nothing.

The fever made her cry. She always cried when she had a fever.

She wished for a thunderstorm to take her home.

But the rains had stopped leaving them in unbearable humid heat.

She wished for Augustus.
Yet she knew even he as a physician couldn't help her.
She longed for Augustus.
But he'd broken her heart.

CHAPTER 103

*H*er hair was soaked with sweat.

Augustus swept the hair off Arabella's forehead.

Minnie pulled the blanket around up to her neck. "Ever time I put these blankets over her, she throws them off. She keeps saying something about letting the fever breath."

"Do you have any quinine?"

"No Sir. Them soldiers. They took everything."

He was one of those soldiers. He knew they used up the household supply of quinine long ago. If only they'd thought to tuck some back for themselves.

Minnie pulled the curtains to and left the room.

Augustus immediately went to the window, threw back the curtains, and opened the window. Arabella had convinced him that fresh air was one of the most important treatments for illness.

He went back to stand next to the bed where she slept.

"Why don't you want the blankets, my dearest?"

Arabella had told him that she worked in a hospital in her

time. Even though she wasn't a medical person, she listened and she learned.

She had to have a reason.

He pulled the blanket back off of her, leaving only the sheet.

The child he'd been tending, the one with malaria, had died. That had been the final straw for Augustus. He wasn't sure what he was going to do yet, but he'd known he need to get back to Arabella.

And here Arabella was with malaria. And he had no quinine.

Without quinine, her chances of survival decreased significantly.

He sat next to the bed and held her hand.

It was all he knew to do.

CHAPTER 104

Arabella woke in the darkness of night. She was so exhausted she could barely move.

Yet she felt safe. Strong arms were wrapped around her.

Augustus.

She was dreaming, of course, as she had so many times before, but it didn't matter. The sensation of being safe and loved was so strong, it pulled at her enough that it might as well be real.

CHAPTER 105

*I*t was just after midnight when Augustus woke with renewed determination to do something – anything – to help Arabella.

If Arabella knew of medicines to cure otherwise incurable maladies, then surely Bradley did, too. They came from the same time.

He found Bradley in the study, writing a letter.

"Bradley Becquerel?" He asked from the doorway.

"Yes?" Bradley had more ink on his fingers than on the paper.

"I'm Augustus Townsend."

"Ah." Bradley leaned back in the chair. Contrary to what Augustus had overhead earlier in the day, Bradley appeared quite calm. "I heard about you, Dr. Townsend."

"Yes. Well, I'm here to ask for your help."

"In what way?" Bradley leaned forward.

"Your niece, Arabella, is ill."

Bradley frowned. "I was told she was under the weather and I could meet her later."

"Of course." Augustus wasn't surprised. Southern propriety

persisted in the oddest of moments. "Actually, I'm afraid it's much more dire than that."

Bradley stood up and came around the desk. "What do you mean?"

"She has malaria."

"Oh God. The mosquitoes. Can you treat it?"

"Mosquitoes?"

Bradley shrugged. "What can you do?"

"I could give her quinine, but we don't have any. I was hoping you knew of some other treatment I don't know about."

"I'm not a doctor."

"Of course. But you're from Arabella's time and… things are different. I know you have medicines. Perhaps you know of something that would help her that I don't know about."

Bradley wiped his hands on a cloth, then pressed the back of his wrist against his forehead. Then he looked back at Augustus. "I personally don't know how to treat it, but I may be able to find out."

Augustus felt his spirits lift for the first time since he'd arrived hours ago. "Anything," he said. "Anything at all."

"We'll need a lantern."

CHAPTER 106

Augustus held the lantern while Bradley climbed several feet into a tree. They'd walked about a hundred yards into the woods, guided only the lantern. The full moon was completely obscured by a thick layer of clouds.

He had no clue what they were doing out here, but Augustus was too desperate to ask questions.

"Hand me the lantern." Bradley reached down and Augustus handed the lantern up. Augustus watched as Bradley pulled a metal box out of a den hole in the tree. He handed the lantern back and Augustus set it down. Then he took the metal box and Bradley climbed back to the ground.

"What is it?" The box was light.

"It's a treasure trove of knowledge." Bradley dusted himself off and took the box from Augustus.

"Let's sit over here." They sat on a fallen log and Bradley opened the box and unwrapped two plates – one metal and one glass. The glass one looked like what Arabella called her cell something-or-other, only bigger.

Bradley pressed a button on the glass one that looked like a mirror and it lit up, just like her smaller one had. Seconds later he touched the screen, changing the image. He swiped his finger along the screen and pictures scrolled up the screen.

He touched one of the images and a book appeared. Just by swiping his finger, the pages moved like magic.

"There's a book in there?" Augustus asked, looked beneath the plate. How could that be?

Bradley grinned. "Sort of. Malaria, right?"

"Yes." Augustus kept his eyes on the screen and watched in amazement as Bradley touched the screen with his fingers and pages moved.

Then a page appeared titled malaria. Together they read the text.

"Malaria comes from mosquitoes," Augustus said. "That makes perfect sense why it's so prevalent here and not up north."

Bradley glanced at him. "No one knows that yet."

"Well I do now! And don't think I won't save lives with this knowledge."

Bradley chuckled and they kept reading.

"Whiskey." They said at the same time.

Bradley turned off the… thing and wrapped it back up. "I'm gonna need to get this in the sun before long."

"The sun gives it energy?"

"Yes."

"I'd like to read that book."

"Sure. After I find my wife and sister and after this war is over, you can do that. You'll be the best damn doctor of the century."

"Speaking of, I've got to get some whiskey in Arabella."

Help me get this back in the tree and we'll go."

Augustus was in awe at the little machines that they'd brought from the future. Whole books in one little device. A little device that was so incomprehensively valuable that it had to remain hidden in metal box in a tree.

And now he had a chance of saving Arabella's life.

CHAPTER 107

*A*rabella sat in her bed propped against a stack of pillows, eating a bowl of soup. Minnie puttered about the room, picking up clothes, towels, and straightening in general.

"That Doctor Augustus, he done brought you back from the dead." Minnie picked up a cloth from the floor, draped it over her arm. "I don't know how he did it, but he nursed you back to health."

Arabella sipped the tomato soup. Augustus. He was back then. She thought she'd imagined it. Her face flushed at where some of her imaginative thoughts had taken her.

Minnie continued to chatter as she moved about the room.

"He came back then," Arabella said out loud.

"Oh yes ma'am. He came back and he didn't give up on you. He stayed right here 'til that fever broke."

"Where is he now?"

Minnie stopped and looked at her, hands on her hips. "Nobody knows."

Arabella set down her spoon. "When did he leave?"

"This morning." Minnie said. "He told me to stay right here

and watch over you. I told him I'll watch over you like a mother hen."

Arabella tuned her out and finished her soup. If Augustus was here, taking care of her, why did he leave before she woke and where had he gone?

She wanted a bath, but she was just too tired to go through the ordeal of having hot water hauled up. Maybe after a nap, she would ask Minnie to bring up some water.

Her eyes drifted closed.

Augustus. Here.

As she drifted asleep, only one thought played in her head.

Augustus had come back.

CHAPTER 108

*A*ugustus sat at the foot of the hollow tree holding the glass device that had a half eaten apple with the word iPad on the back.

He'd imitated Bradley's behavior and had spent the morning reading about the future.

The iPad contained an entire set of encyclopedias. He'd read about automobiles, airplanes, and computers. There was so much information. So much had changed in the past one hundred fifty years. The entire world was different. He'd read a few things about medicine, but most of what he read required machinery to implement.

He had just found a chapter on the American Civil War when the iPad went blank. It was perplexing because he'd been sitting in the sunlight specifically to make sure it had enough power.

Since Bradley hadn't explained anything about the other device, Augustus left it alone. He carefully wrapped the iPad back in the cloth and returned it to the tree.

There would be hell to pay if he'd broken it. And rightly so.

A device that held all the knowledge from 2018 back had no price and could never be replaced.

But now Augustus had validated his decision. He would do whatever it took to be with Arabella, even if it meant going with her to the future.

He'd been surprised she was still here. He'd thought that if he left her, she would be free of his love and free to return to her own time.

But he hadn't been able to stay away from her.

Perhaps merely being apart hadn't been enough to break their bond. Even with him under the pretense of never coming back.

Perhaps fate knew better.

Now all he had to do was to convince Arabella that he'd walked away from her in order to save her.

He scoffed at himself.

His sister was right. Men could be idiots.

CHAPTER 109

rabella went downstairs and found her father in the study.

He jumped up and drew her into a hug when he saw her standing in the doorway. "Arabella. I thought I had lost you again."

"What happened?"

"You took ill with malaria and we had no quinine to give you."

"I could have died."

"Yes, but Augustus gave you whiskey until the fever broke."

She put a hand over her eyes. "That explains the headache. Where is he?"

"I don't know."

"So he left again."

"I don't know ma petite cherie."

She collapsed into one of the two large chairs in his office. This trip downstairs had been more difficult than she expected. She was weak from the malaria. And the afternoon heat didn't help.

"Your uncle was here." Charles sat in the chair next to hers.

"Uncle?" Her brain was still foggy.

"Bradley. But he left to search for Camille and your mother."

"Oh. Good." She wasn't sure what the implications of this were. Right now she was more concerned about Augustus swooping in to treat her malaria, then disappearing again. "Why was Augustus here?"

Charles scrunched his eyebrows. "He didn't say."

"It's odd, don't you think?"

"A little. But men do odd things for the women they love."

She scoffed. "Those things don't usually involve running off with no explanation."

"You're right."

Arabella froze. And turned her eyes toward the door. Augustus stood there, a half smile on his face.

"I'd like the opportunity to explain."

She glanced at her father.

"I'll leave you two alone."

"No." Augustus stepped forward. "I'd like you to understand, too." He went to Arabella and knelt in front of her. He took her hand in his and kissed her palm.

"I love you."

She inhaled sharply. Words she had longed to hear for so long.

He glanced at Charles. "Sir, I'm in love with your daughter."

Charles watched him in silence. He turned back to her.

"Arabella, I didn't want to take you from the life you were accustomed to. If I was the one keeping you here, I wanted you to be safe. So you could return to a time when there were medicines that could actually save lives."

She shook her head. What was he saying? That he loved her so he was setting her free? She'd always thought that saying was nonsense. Relationships should be easy. If they weren't easy, move on. What was the point?

Of course, that's what had gotten her in trouble with Matthew. It had been easy and she had simply let it slide.

But right now wasn't about the past. Right now was about Augustus kneeling in front of her declaring his love.

"Augustus…"

"Wait. I apologize for leaving you the way I did. I was hoping that you would be able to return to your own time and I also thought that I could stay away from you." He took her other hand and held both her hands in his. "But I couldn't. I couldn't stay away from you."

Arabella blinked back the tears that threatened to spill down her cheeks.

"Sir. May I have permission to ask for your daughter's hand. I'll understand if-"

"Yes."

Augustus smiled. "Arabella. It matters not to me whether we're in this time or your time. I only want to be with you. If you're happier in the future, I'll go there with you."

She couldn't stop the tears. "I don't think it works that way." Her breath hitched.

"However it works, I want to live the rest of my life with you. Will you marry me?"

"Yes," she breathed, glancing at her father. "But only if you agree to stay here in this time. Here with my family."

He pulled her in his arms. Kissed her forehead, her eyelids, the tears from her cheeks. "Wherever you are, that's where I'll be happy."

"This calls for a whiskey," Charles said.

Arabella groaned. "Please. No more whiskey."

EPILOGUE

Six Months Later

Arabella lay with her head in Augustus' lap on the porch swing. He gently rocked the swing and toyed with the ends of her hair. She was pleasantly exhausted from a day of chores – today they had made candles. Dipping the wicks into the hot wax had required a lot of tedious repetition.

Her father and Augustus had spent the day chopping wood and repairing a chicken coop.

She looked over at her father, Charles Becquerel. He was sitting a few feet away in a chair, smoking a cigar. He held the book he'd been reading until the dusk took away the light. It still felt surreal to think she was here with her father. The father she thought had died when she was an infant. And in all truthfulness, Vaughn hadn't lied to her. When Vaughn had brought her through time, her parents had been dead to her.

Though Charles had written his wife, Ericka, several times, he hadn't heard back from her. There was no way to know if she had even gotten the letters. Travel was dangerous and the mail was erratic as the war waged around them. Even after

Bradley went in search of them, they'd had no word from any of them.

Augustus had requested permission to resign from the Confederate army and it had been granted on the grounds that he was needed as a physician on the home front. His fear of being found treasonous had been unfounded. Ironically, even as he had resigned, he still served. Their reputation as an unofficial hospital continued and wounded men still flocked to their doorstep on a regular basis.

The air had a chill, but Arabella didn't mind. It was nearing Christmas-time and Arabella was with Augustus, the man she had fallen in love with. He spoke of visiting with his family after the war, but assured her that he would not be leaving the Becquerel estate again without her. Arabella had yet to determine what that meant for her, but she was content.

Arabella had developed an ear for anyone coming down their driveway. She leaned up and stared down the road and just as she had anticipated, they had a visitor.

She watched as a horse and buggy came into view. The horse was ragged and bony, but that was to be expected. The whole south was ragged and bony.

What was unexpected was that two women were in the buggy. The men followed her gaze and the three of them watched as they came closer.

Charles stood up silently, his eyes glued to the road, and went to the edge of the porch. Arabella sat up, watching her father as much as she watched the buggy coming down the road. She had no more than discerned that the buggy held females, than Charles had bolted down the front steps.

Though his limp was evident, he moved quickly and stopped the buggy before it touched the circle drive. Then one of the women was out of the buggy and in his arms. They held each other as the seconds ticked past.

Then the woman said something to the other one who then

whipped the reins and continued toward the house. Charles held the woman's hands and after talking briefly, they started walking toward the house, still hand in hand.

Augustus went out to meet the woman driving the buggy. Arabella followed.

The woman secured the reins and allowed Augustus to lift her from the buggy. Her dress was torn and soiled, but of obvious good quality. She wore a hoop skirt in similar size to Arabella's. Even though she looked tired, it was obvious that she was stunningly beautiful.

Safely on the ground, she turned to them. "Hello. I'm Camille Becquerel."

Arabella and Augustus looked at each other. Arabella grinned and went to hug her. "You're Uncle Bradley's wife."

"Yes. How did you know?"

"I've heard Charles speak of you."

"I'm afraid you have me at a disadvantage."

Arabella took a deep breath. "I'm Arabella."

Camille gasped and stared at her. She put a hand over her mouth, her eyes wide with obvious surprise. "The missing baby."

Arabella smiled. "It's seems I've been found."

"I can't believe it. I was holding you. And then I handed you over to Vaughn and then you were both… just vanished. Ericka never admitted to blaming me, but I always felt it was my fault."

"It was no one's fault. It just happened."

"But… you're here." She looked from Arabella to Augustus and back again.

Arabella turned just as she heard someone running toward them.

The woman stopped a few feet from her. Arabella blinked.

And she looked into the eyes of an older version of herself.

ANOTHER EPILOGUE

May 1865

Arabella ran a hand along her swollen belly. The end of the war had come. Finally. But nothing had changed for them. Except maybe higher taxes, but somehow the men were managing.

The women stayed busy managing the household. Camille's daughter, Becca, had returned home after her husband was killed in the war. And she brought her own infant with her.

Arabella's heart broke every time she thought about Becca's story. They had been newlyweds when the war started. Last year, her husband had returned home for three days. Three whole days and now Becca was a single mom. Or as Camille said, a widow.

Arabella was thankful that Augustus remained on the home front. Together they took care of those wounded, physically and mentally.

He'd shown her the iPad that Bradley had hidden in the tree and she'd shown him how to charge it with the solar panel. They'd spent hours reading together and talking about the information stored on it.

Arabella and Ericka were outside hanging clothes on a line strung between two trees. Camille sat at a tub, scrubbing clothes on a washboard. Over the past few months, she'd grown quiet and carried a sadness with her. She didn't say it, but everyone knew that she feared the worst for Bradley and mourned his absence.

"What do you miss the most about home?" Ericka asked. They'd tacitly agreed to refer to the future as *home.* "Right now for me it's got to be the washer and dryer."

Arabella laughed. "That's easy. For me it's my cell phone."

"The cell phone does everything now, doesn't it?"

"You have no idea. I even had an app to tell me if I was brushing my teeth right."

Ericka paused and stared at her. "Seriously?"

"I'm not kidding." Arabella froze and watched when she saw a soldier coming out of the woods. There was a path that led directly to the river from here, but not too many people knew about it. He was a ragged looking soldier – his clothes were tattered and he was barefoot.

Ericka followed her gaze. "Another one…"

But Arabella heard something in her voice that sounded different…

She dropped the shirt she was holding back into the basket and took a step forward. Then she glanced toward Camille, but Camille's eyes were focused on the washboard where she scrubbed a shirt.

The soldier kept coming toward them.

Camille looked in their direction, doubtless alerted by their sudden silence. She then turned around and followed their gaze.

Ericka's hand flew to her mouth. "It's Bradley," she whispered.

Arabella watched as recognition dawned on Camille's face a second later. She sat very still and watched as Bradley neared.

She sat still as a statue until Bradley stood directly in front of her. Then she was in his arms.

"Come on," Ericka said. "Come meet your uncle."

Augustus and Charles came out the back door.

"Hey," Charles said. "It's time to…."

"Let's go finish the washing up for them." Augustus said before he saw Bradley.

Then all four of them were standing around Camille and Bradley. Tears were streaming down Camille's face and Bradley grinned and swept her off her feet in a circle.

Augustus took Arabella's hand and pulled her against him. "Uncle Bradley made it home," he whispered into her ear.

"I think you're right. I told you he wasn't on the list."

They'd searched Civil War records on the iPad books, but hadn't located Bradley's name anywhere. Of course, having internet would have helped.

Bradley hugged his sister and was introduced to his niece, Arabella.

Arabella soon found herself in a huge bear hug. Bradley may have looked a little ragged from a distance, but he still had his strength.

"Careful," Augustus warned. "The baby."

"I'm always careful," Bradley said, releasing Arabella back to her doting husband's care.

Arabella watched the little family, husband and wives, brothers and sisters, and felt a strong surge of belongingness sweep over her.

Family.

She may have grown up in another time, but this was where she belonged.

No matter what time period it was, home was where and *when* her family was.

Right here. Right now.

She turned and looked up at Augustus – into his handsome face and eyes filled with love.

With one hand on her stomach and the other on her cheek, he pressed his lips against hers.

"This is where we belong," she murmured against his lips.

"Together." He kissed her on the cheek. "No matter when."

Want more time travel?
How about a bonus short story?

GET MY BONUS SHORT STORY
https://BookHip.com/DTSKGNJ

Read more about Vaughn and Jonathan in Once Upon a Christmas.

Turn the page for a preview of
Once Upon a Christmas...

ONCE UPON A CHRISTMAS PREVIEW

December 1969

aughn Dupre woke disoriented. It was nothing unusual. She woke disoriented every day.

She'd fallen asleep after an evening spent listening to Nathaniel read to his five-year-old son, Beau. His three-year-old daughter, Abigail, had already fallen asleep snuggled in her mother's lap. While the parents tucked their two children into bed, Vaughn had gone to her bedroom and crawled beneath the warm blankets.

Now, as she lay here with her eyes closed, she tried to sort out what was different. The sheet pulled over her head smelled… masculine.

Her eyes flew open. Her bed had smelled clean and feminine when she'd fallen asleep last night. Had she somehow ended up in Nathaniel and Martha's bed? She was certain she had not. Yet… the masculine scent was unmistakable. She only knew this because she had spent the last two months as the nanny for Nathaniel and Martha, which sometimes included doing household chores like making beds.

She slowly lowered the sheet and cautiously opened one eye. She gasped.

This was not the room she had fallen asleep in. Gone was the little dresser with the flowers she and Abigail had picked yesterday. Gone was the nightstand with the candles.

Instead, the bed was turned so that she faced the window. The curtains were mere strips of white cloth hanging from the ceiling. Gone were the thick velvet drapes that had been drawn closed when she had fallen asleep.

Suddenly, a loud buzzing filled the air. She threw a hand over her ears and ducked back below the sheets. It sounded like a giant bee.

When the noise stopped, she realized it wasn't an insect in her ear or even in her room.

Quiet as a mouse, she got up and slid off the bed onto the floor. As her toes touched the cool wood, she glanced down. At least her night gown had not changed.

She walked to the window and peeked out.

The buzzing started again.

She gasped and jumped back, her heart nearly jumping out of her chest.

The buzzing stopped and was followed by a loud clatter.

She waited. This time, steeling herself, she went back to the window and peeked out again.

A man, his back to the window, stood below. He was wearing blue trousers and a white shirt. His dark hair was short. He stacked some boards across two wooden platforms, then picked up one long board and turned toward the house.

She moved closer to the tall window, so she could see him better.

As though he sensed her, he looked up and saw her standing there watching him, a scowl on his face.

She froze. Her hands fisted into the cotton of her nightgown.

His scowl changed into a grin. He hoisted the board onto his shoulder, then disappeared inside the house.

Vaughn inhaled quickly and lifted her gaze to the grounds. She was facing the back of the house. The clothesline was gone, as were the clothes she had hung out last night to dry. To her right sat an odd-looking buggy in bright red.

There were no fields of cotton. Just trees where the cotton fields had been yesterday.

She moved closer, grasping the curtain in her right hand.

She jumped back when the grandfather clock began to toll the hour. And faced the room.

Seven o'clock.

Everything was the same, yet different.

It made no sense that she was would be in Nathaniel and Martha's chambers.

She listened closely, but didn't hear the children. Usually by now, they would be up, running down the hallway, getting ready for breakfast.

Then she heard hammering from somewhere inside the house. She needed to get to her room and get dressed so that she could figure out what was going on.

She made her way to the door, then dashed down the hallway, the sound of her footsteps disguised by the hammering. She went into her room and closed the door.

Her heart raced.

The bed was made, but she didn't recognize the green blanket tucked neatly across the top. She'd left her dress draped across the back of a chair next to the bed. Not only was her dress missing, but the chair was gone as well.

She went to the bureau and threw open the doors. Other than a blanket folded neatly and sitting on the top shelf, the bureau was empty.

A wave of panic shot through her, and she ran her hands along her nightgown.

She had nothing to wear.

She turned, and her gaze fell on her reflection in the mirror. She saw a panic-stricken girl dressed in a white shift, her brunette hair cascading around her shoulders. She hurried to the dresser and searched through the drawers, but there was no brush.

She sat on the stool and put her face in her hands.

Then she took a deep breath. After everything she'd been through, she could surely figure this out. She sat up and squared her shoulders. The noise downstairs had grown quiet.

Perhaps that man could help her.

Keep reading Once Upon a Christmas…

Kathryn Kaleigh is the author of sixty-eight novels, over one hundred short stories, and many collections.

kathrynkaleigh.com